Snow

Catherine Farnes

JOURNEY
BOOKS™
Greenville, South Carolina

Library of Congress Cataloging-in-Publication Data

Farnes, Catherine, 1964-
    Snow / Catherine Farnes
    p. cm.
    Summary: Sixteen-year-old Stephanie, a visually impaired albino, gets help in adjusting to a new high school when she befriends several Christian kids, who point her toward a deep and satisfying relationship with God.
    ISBN 1-57924-199-9
    I. Title.
PZ7.F238265 Sn 1999
    [Fic]—dc21   98-40785
                                                              CIP
                                                              AC

Snow

Edited by Debbie L. Parker
Designed by Duane A. Nichols
Cover by Mary Ann Lumm

© 1999 Bob Jones University Press
Greenville, South Carolina 29614

ISBN 1-57924-199-9

15   14   13   12   11   10   9   8   7   6   5   4   3   2   1

For Sarah Lyda
For Jerry Baker
For Richard Reuben

Contents

Hast thou entered into the treasures of the snow?
—Job 38:22

Chapter One

I stayed in the entryway for several moments, letting my eyes adjust to the dimmer light inside the school. Reluctantly, but knowing that I had no choice, I tightened my hold on the strap of my book bag and stepped into the crowded hallway. I would be noticed. No question.

My first day at Canyon Street High.

It was March of my junior year in high school, and here I was, starting all over again. A new city halfway across the country. A new school.

"I'm Stephanie Teale," I told the woman behind the counter in the main office. "Someone was supposed to meet me and show me around the building this morning before classes?" Since she seemed momentarily powerless to function beyond the ability to stare, I looked down at the countertop and stated the obvious. "I'm new here."

"Just a minute."

Then she left me standing there.

"This'll be a great chance for you to get out into the real world, Stephanie," my mother had told me when I'd hinted at some discomfort about moving. Then she had smiled and tucked a loose strand of my hair behind my ear. "Maybe you'll be able to broaden someone's horizons."

I didn't want to broaden horizons. I wanted to be normal. Like everyone else.

SNOW

The woman returned with a man who introduced himself as Mr. Parisch—the Special Needs Counselor.

I did not need a *special needs counselor*. I just needed someone to show me around the building . . . which is exactly what I told Mr. Parisch . . . and coldly.

"Hey," he said, "I'm here to serve. Whatever the need."

Embarrassed by his easy response to my bluntness, I apologized. "I guess I'm a little nervous."

"Everyone gets nervous in new situations," he said.

Did they? I wondered.

I followed Mr. Parisch around the first floor and then the second of Canyon Street High, thinking how strange it felt to be in such a new building, and one with so many students.

"So . . . you went to a school for the blind in New England?" Mr. Parisch asked as we left one of the school's three computer rooms.

The caution in his tone amused me. "Yes. I went to a blind school."

"How'd you like it?"

I shrugged. "I liked it a lot better than the public school I went to every afternoon."

"Why?"

"You're counseling," I jokingly warned. "I don't need a counselor, remember?"

He stayed silent.

Slowly, I admitted the truth, just to see what Mr. Parisch would say. "I don't like getting teased."

"And you were teased in the public school."

It wasn't a question. The fact that I'd be teased was obvious. Even though my visual impairment might not be immediately evident—I didn't use a white cane, wear dark glasses, or have a guide dog—I *was* very visibly an albino.

White hair. White skin. Eyes that, though blue, looked purple half the time.

I laughed. "I have to admit that some people did come up with some good ones occasionally."

Mr. Parisch didn't ask me to elaborate, and I was glad for that. At least I wouldn't have to remember out loud. *Frosty. Snow White. White Bat Woman. Vanilla with Hair. Casper. Whitey Ford* (Who was he, anyway?). And the most annoying, *Albo Annie.*

"Well," Mr. Parisch said after a moment, "I wish I could tell you that nobody here will harass you, but—"

Just then, someone—a boy, of course—ran by us yelling, "Albino! Albino! Albino! There *is* life on the moon!"

I looked at Mr. Parisch. He looked at me. Both of us had to laugh.

"Life on the moon?" I shook my head. Now that was a new one.

"Got to give him credit for perfect timing," joked Mr. Parisch.

"Yeah. No kidding. And for creativity."

Mr. Parisch shook his head slowly, and his expression turned serious. "Don't worry. I'll catch up with him later."

I nodded politely.

"So . . ."

There was that caution in his tone again. I waved it away. "Oh, go ahead and counsel," I said. "I might be a blubbering heap in your office this afternoon anyway . . . assuming I can find it, that is." I had noticed during our tour that the numbers on the walls above each doorway were not large enough for me to read.

Mr. Parisch laughed. "I get the feeling you're going to do just fine, Stephanie." He led me into the gymnasium. "You seem to handle life with humor. That is always a plus."

"Yeah, well, pigment would be an even bigger plus."

He nodded, though he seemed unsure of how to take my attempt at humor. Finally, though, he said, "There are women who pay—"

"I know. I know." I raised my hand to interrupt him. "Thousands of dollars to have hair my color. I know."

I guess he could tell that such knowledge comforted me not at all. He said, "Stephanie, I believe that God made each of us unique. Like the different jewels in a treasure."

"Unique is one thing," I said. "Weird and ugly is another. Like the rocks in a gravel parking lot. And I don't believe in God."

He said, "I guess you've never looked closely at parking lot rocks."

I said nothing.

He took me back into the main hallway, and we stopped in front of a narrow section of lockers. "We've assigned you a locker with a padlock so that you don't have to fight the combination lock."

"That was very . . . politically correct of you." I smiled. "It was also thoughtful. Thanks." I had practiced with a combination lock at home in preparation for this day, and the inevitability of having to be seen with my face right next to the lock, squinting at the numbers, had actually given me nightmares.

I took the small key from Mr. Parisch, unlocked the padlock on the locker in front of me, pulled it off, and opened the locker to hang my jacket inside. "Is it too late for me to try out for the track team?"

Mr. Parisch shook his head. "Nope. They're just getting started for the season. What events do you do?"

He didn't sound surprised that I'd be interested in or able to run track. I appreciated that. "The mile."

After telling me when and where I could find the girls' coach and reminding me that I could come to his office any time, Mr. Parisch left me alone to fend for myself and find my first class.

As I walked along the hall, trying to pretend that I didn't notice the way other kids stopped talking to one another to watch me walk by, I wondered if I'd ever really fit in anywhere.

In New England, at the school for the blind that I had attended since kindergarten, I had usually been among a minority of students whose only disability was visual impairment. Though I enjoyed a lot of success there (and no teasing!), everyone had such individual needs that it was difficult to feel like part of a group. To fit in.

And then there was my mother's—the "Real World." The real world of fully sighted people. Where calculators did not talk. Where most people could drive. Where everything from menus in fast-food restaurants to the written signs above restroom doors would challenge me . . . and sometimes force me to ask for help—which I hated to do. The real world where I would always be one-in-fifteen-thousand. A genetic abnormality.

Someone to stare at.

But there was a place where I could belong . . . even if I couldn't exactly fit in. One place where I actually enjoyed the knowledge that people were watching me. A place where I had always been able to compete with, if not outperform, other girls my age.

The track.

The mile.

I had a computer monitor box full (and my computer monitor was, of course, among the largest available) of ribbons and medals from races against fully sighted athletes as well as those with visual impairment similar to my own. I loved to run. I loved to train. And, most of all, I loved to compete . . . and win. I knew that running wouldn't get me a job in my mother's "Real World," but it gave me a lot of satisfaction in mine.

On the track it didn't matter what color my hair was, or whether or not I could recognize the person beside me. All that mattered was getting to the tape first. And I, *Albo Annie, Bleach,*

SNOW

Whiteylocks, or whatever else anyone wanted to call me, could usually do that.

As I slid into the seat my first-hour teacher assigned me and then opened the textbook to see if I'd be able to read it without my magnifying glass, I decided that no matter how horrible the day turned out to be, I was going to find the track coach after school and earn myself a spot on Canyon Street High's varsity team.

Chapter Two

After warming up with some stretches and a few sprints, I stood near the starting line and waited for the coach. She had told me that I'd probably get a place on the team no matter how quickly or slowly I ran the 1600 meters because participation in track seemed to be low this year, but I wanted her to time me anyway. I wanted her to take me seriously right from the start.

But as I stood there waiting for her, I began to feel nervous. What if the higher elevation here in Colorado affected my running somehow? I hadn't thought of that.

"Ready, Miss Teale?"

Not really, but . . . I smiled at the coach. "Sure."

"I figured I'd get some of the other milers out here with you. Make it feel like a race." She watched my face for a reaction. "Okay?"

"Sure."

Five girls stepped onto the track with me. One of them mumbled a hello, but the others did not acknowledge me—except for a couple of quiet snickers. Either these girls were extremely fierce competitors, or they were just plain rude. I suspected the latter, but I smiled at them and told them my name.

A couple of them returned the courtesy.

The coach blew a whistle to clear the track. Most of the kids, boys and girls alike, lingered in the infield to watch the six of us run. Many of them called out encouragement. *Go Kelly! Go Shaunie! Go Brit!* Most of the cheers, though, were for Dana—one of the girls who hadn't introduced herself to me. If she had, I would have moved to position myself right beside her. Clearly, she was the team favorite in the girls' 1600 . . . the person I'd want to stay with through the first three laps of the track and then hopefully pass in the final 300 meters.

But I didn't know who Dana was, so I'd have to run my own mile and hope it would prove to be the fastest.

We lined up, waited for the whistle, and, when we heard it, we started running. All six of us stayed together through the first half of the run, but we started to spread out as runners began to fall back or pull ahead. I stayed back a bit, waiting to see which girl seemed to be the most serious about getting into the lead, and then quickened my pace to catch her.

Each breath burned slightly more than it usually did at this point in a race, probably because of the higher elevation. I began to focus on the sound and rhythm of my steps on the track, ignoring the different pacing of the two girls I passed, to put myself right behind the leader. I stayed close enough to her to hear her shoelaces hitting the tops of her shoes each time she'd pick her foot up off the track . . . right behind her . . . until the last 110 meters, when I stepped out to the side and began to sprint.

But she clearly did not plan to be passed.

People were shouting, but I was no longer paying attention to what they were saying. I could see the end of the straightaway. The coach standing there. The girl's white shoes hitting the track in pace with mine. Even with me.

And that's how the run ended.

Dead even.

Well, it was good enough for a spot on the team . . . and to earn some measure of politeness in the form of a "Nice run!" or two from the other runners as well as from the coach.

But the girl who'd finished with me? She wouldn't even look at me. I tried to talk with her, to ask her how long she'd been running, but she kept walking along the infield as if she hadn't heard me. I knew she had heard me, though, because when a boy ran up behind us calling her name—*Dana*, she instantly turned to face him—smile and everything.

"Hi, Wayne," she said, her tone thick enough with *You're so cute* that I had to pretend to cough just to squelch the urge to laugh aloud.

"Good run," he said to her. "Are you going to the weight room now?"

Dana shook her head. "I'm going to go run the bleachers."

"I'll go with you."

And they disappeared into the sunset. Literally. The sun in the western sky was just above the horizon, and its brightness blinded me whenever I looked its way.

I considered going to the stands to run bleachers, but decided against it. Unsafe. I thought about the weight room. Boring. Since the coach had told me that I could begin training with the team tomorrow, I decided to leave. I'd gotten my place on the team. I'd shown these people that I could run. True, I hadn't beaten Dana, but she hadn't beaten me either. The other kids on the team might still ignore me, but they could no longer discount me or laugh at me.

I stopped at the edge of the track before crossing it to make sure it was clear of runners. To my right, empty track. To my left . . . the sun. I held my hand above my eyes to shield them from the glare, but it didn't do a whole lot of good. I still couldn't see.

Well, here's hoping they're not drilling the boys' 400 right now, I thought as I stepped out onto the track. Nothing was more annoying than seeing some loser in your lane when you were running full speed and—

—and being unable to slow down or stop before you plowed right into him.

I barely felt the boy run into me, but I sure felt the ground when I hit it. Several feet away from the track. On my backside. With everyone in the stands staring down at me . . . laughing.

Suddenly a hand grabbed mine, and I was gently pulled to my feet. A boy only slightly taller than me looked straight at me as he slowly let go of my hand. "I'm really sorry," he said. "Are you all right?"

"I'm fine," I said. I looked down at the dirt where I had fallen. "It was my fault. I'm sorry."

One of the boys' coaches jogged toward us. "Is she all right?" he asked, sounding more irritated than concerned.

"I'm fine," I assured him.

After a tense pause, the coach said, "All right, come on, guys. We'll start again."

Several groans came from the group of boys who had stopped on the track to see what had happened.

"Look before you cross the track next time," the coach said to me.

The kids in the stands started laughing as if this were the most hilarious thing they had heard all year, but the boy who'd run into me glared at the coach. "She did look," he said. "I saw her. The sun was right in her eyes."

"I'm surprised the reflection off her didn't blind you, Nathan," someone shouted to him.

"The preschool's across the street," he yelled back. "It's the building with the big yellow ABC's on the window. You can't miss it." Then, quietly to me, he said, "Don't listen to them. They don't know anything."

I looked only halfway up at him. "I'm sorry."

"Don't worry about it." He waved away my apology. "I saw you finish the mile with Dana Cullen," he said. "Good job. I've never seen anyone finish that close to her."

"Let's go!" his coach shouted from the track.

"See you later," the boy said to me. Then he ran to catch up with the other runners who were heading back toward the starting line.

I hurried across the track, forcing myself not to look down at the ground as I walked past the stands where several kids were still laughing —probably at *me*. The temptation to let myself feel like an absolute loser pressed down on me with its familiar persuasiveness, but I ignored it. This time. Because as soon as I pulled open the door and stepped inside the school, leaving the stands, the track, and the laughter behind me, I made a resolution. A commitment to prove to myself—and to every person in those stands who had laughed at me—that I was not an absolute loser.

"I've never seen anyone finish that close to her," the boy—Nathan—had said. Well, sometime during this track season, no matter how hard I had to work to do it, I was going to finish ahead of Dana Cullen.

Chapter Three

"So, how was school, honey?" Ma asked me as soon as I walked through the door. It sounded as if she were in the kitchen, possibly reorganizing the cupboards again.

Poor Dad. His house wasn't his own anymore.

I dropped my book bag on the floor beside the coat tree and walked slowly through the dining room, into the kitchen. "Oh, you know, Ma," I said. "It was school."

"Did you make any new friends?"

"Yeah, Ma. Thousands." I sat in one of Dad's oak chairs at the cluttered kitchen table and ran the tip of my forefinger across the corner of the telephone book. "I got a spot on the track team."

Ma sat beside me, smiling. "Was there any doubt you would?"

I ignored her attempt to make me feel good about myself. "How was your day?" I asked. She'd worked full-time in New England, and I knew that staying at home here in Colorado—since Dad could afford for her not to work—was an adjustment for her.

"Well," she said with a sigh, "I rewallpapered the utility room and finished that book I started three years ago."

"And is that lasagna I smell?"

She smiled and nodded.

"Shouldn't Dad be here soon?"

Ma glanced at the clock on the microwave. "Any minute."

My parents. I did admire them for deciding—especially since it had been seven years since their divorce—to try to put their marriage back together. And even though I had to respect the sacrifices each of them seemed to be willing to make to give their second chance a serious shot at success, I couldn't help feeling a little scared. What if it didn't work out? What if Ma ended up on her own again? Would she stay here in Colorado or return to New England? And what of the bitterness between my parents? Wouldn't it be even greater after a second failure? A second hope wasted?

Me? I'd be seventeen in a few months. I certainly didn't need my parents to be together now—not for my sake, anyway. But I hoped they'd be able to make it work this time.

"Do you know where your father keeps his camera?" Ma asked me. "I wanted to drive out and take some pictures of the mountains for Grandma and Grandpa today, but I couldn't find a camera. Mine or his."

I knew exactly where Dad kept his camera. I knew exactly where Dad kept everything—and so did Dad. "In the top of the hall closet upstairs," I told Ma.

"Great. Thanks." She hurried out of the room and up the stairs.

Though school was definitely going to be an adjustment for me, living in this house was not. I'd spent three weeks here every summer since the divorce. I had my own room, which I had decorated in peach and hunter green. Though I rarely went there, I knew the way to the public pool, a grocery store, a park, a library, and anywhere else I might want to go. I'd even chosen the household pet a couple of summers earlier—a parrot named Shakespeare.

Still, I'd never exactly thought of the place as home. It was always Dad's house. I felt at home whenever I was visiting . . . but that was the thing . . . I was always visiting. I lived with Ma. In New England.

Until a week ago, that is.

"You were right, Stephanie," Ma announced as she came back downstairs. I knew she was wearing hiking boots without even having to look at her feet. Hard rubber soles and old wood steps made a very definite noise in combination. "The camera was right where you said it'd be."

"Glad to help," I said, trying to sound enthusiastic.

Ma set the camera on top of the china cabinet—and I knew she'd forget where she'd put it and drive herself crazy all the next day looking for it—and sat beside me again. "I know this is hard on you, Stephanie, moving here." She placed her hand over mine. "I . . . I appreciate how grown-up you're being about it all."

The first thing that came to mind was how un-grown-up I'd felt that afternoon at the track when I'd wanted to cry because everyone had laughed at me, but I said, "I want this to work out for you guys," because that was true too.

"I'm glad you didn't decide to stay in the dormitory until the end of the year." She smiled and stood up to start clearing the table.

"Oh," I said, "I knew you'd need me around to help you find things."

Laughing a little, she nodded. Then she stopped working to look right at me. "I need you around for a lot more than that."

Now it was my turn to nod. The truth was, I had thought very seriously about staying in the dorm at the school for the blind until the end of the school year. Both of my parents had assured me that they'd understand, and all my friends and teachers were urging me to do it. The school staff was even going to arrange for me to have a room to myself. But I knew that I'd never be content with myself if I abandoned Ma to making such a big change by herself. She'd always been there for me. In so many different ways. She wasn't the perfect mother—but who was? Choosing to come to Colorado right away with her had been the right thing to do.

Canyon Street High, and all.

Unfortunately, knowing that I had done the right thing by my mother was not going to make life any easier for me at school. But I had track. And a goal there to work toward. It would be okay.

When the front door opened, Shakespeare started squawking, "Dr. Teale! Dr. Teale! *Rrraaaww.* It's five-thirty!" (which is what he said whenever Dad walked through the front door, even at 9:00 A.M.). He didn't quit until Dad had passed by him on his way into the kitchen.

"Hey, guys," Dad said. "Smells great in here. What's cooking?" He set his briefcase beside the china cabinet—where he always put it after work—loosened his tie, and started helping Ma pull dishes from the cupboard to set the table.

I poured everyone a glassful of white grape juice while Ma and Dad got dinner on the table. We took our time about eating, enjoying the food and the easy way conversation kept coming. Everyone laughed a lot, even me. When we finished, Dad asked me if I felt like going for a short walk.

"Sure," I said. It would be good to get a little exercise. Maybe my legs wouldn't stiffen up quite so much after running for the first time in over a week.

We walked to the corner convenience store, where Dad bought us each a milk shake, and then headed up St. John's Lane toward Bethel Park.

"So, was school as horrible as you thought it was going to be?" Dad asked me.

"Worse," I said, laughing but serious. I told him about stepping onto the track in front of that boy—Nathan Whoever-He-Was.

"Did you get hurt?"

The concern in Dad's tone was as misplaced as my mother's car keys usually were. I laughed. "No. Not the way you mean, anyway."

"Kids are cruel because they're insecure."

And hadn't I heard *that* line a thousand times before! I said, "Yeah, Dad. I know."

"My pastor's son runs track at your school," Dad said after a few quiet moments. "I can't imagine he'd laugh at you."

"*Everyone* laughed, Dad," I said, irritated. "Don't be so naive." I had never met a Christian who was actually different than everyone else . . . except my father.

I tossed my empty cup into a trash bin as we entered Bethel Park. "Look, Dad," I said, "I know that your life has totally changed since you decided you were a Christian last year . . . "

In fact, wasn't that the whole reason he'd given up his *I'm-the-good-looking-wealthy-bachelor* lifestyle to try to do right by Ma after all these years—writing her letters at first and then flying up to New England whenever he could to "court" her again until she decided to remarry him? Wasn't it because of his new-found faith that he'd opened a savings account for me for college in the amount of all the child support he hadn't gotten around to sending—enough to cover every penny he was supposed to have paid over the years plus interest? And how about the fact that he was actually decent to live with now, day in and day out? All of it, he said, was because he was trying to live for God now instead of for himself.

Yes, my father's life had changed. But . . . some pastor's kid? Some teenager?

"Dad, I've known kids who say they're Christians who are just as rude as anyone else. They don't call names, maybe, but they're just as worried about who they're seen with."

"I guess I can see that being true," Dad admitted. "But I don't think it's fair for you to judge all Christians by those who maybe haven't been strong enough to do the right thing." He shrugged. "God *can* change people, Stephanie, and make them into who He wants them to be." He didn't say "Look at me!," probably because he knew he didn't have to.

The difference in his life said it.

Still . . . my skepticism held firm. "Dad, even though it probably would take something supernatural to make anyone 'normal' really accept me . . . I don't see it happening that way. I just . . . " I paused to decide whether or not I really wanted to aim a conversation with my father in this direction. He hadn't preached at me yet, and I didn't want to get him started! But I couldn't avoid the subject forever. "I just don't believe in God, Dad."

There. I'd said it. Now all there was to do was wait to see how he'd respond. Tears? Anger? A two-hour lecture on the virtues of faith?

I readied myself for at least one of the above, maybe all, but all Dad said was, "Neither did I." Then he sat on the bench of a shiny red picnic table, waited for me to settle in across from him, and started talking about his plans for a summer vacation along the Pacific Coast.

I guessed that he meant for those three words to speak for themselves.

And the trouble was . . . they did.

Chapter Four

My second day at Canyon Street High began in much the same way as the first, but it quickly became even more annoying because now I wasn't just *the albino* to laugh at—I was the albino who sat on the track (though hardly anyone worded it so discreetly). I tried not to let it bother me. I really did. But by the time I entered my third-hour class, Choir, I began to think seriously about sitting on my hands lest one of them fly up and smack someone before I could stop it.

But I knew I wouldn't hit anyone. I'd just sit there and listen to the snickers, the stupid comments, and all the whispered sympathy for Nathan.

What else could I do?

Telling rude kids to shut up rarely accomplished anything. Neither did telling myself that they were only teasing me because of their own low self-esteem. The only thing that did seem to work sometimes was ignoring them—or at least making it appear that way to them—until they grew bored and moved on.

Unfortunately, with only two-and-a-half months until the end of the school year, the chances of that happening were minimal.

I pulled a piece of sheet music from the folder I found under my chair and began to study it. Since there was only one folder for every two students and I'd have to share the music with whoever sat beside me, and since I'd never be able to see it when I held it out in front of us, I decided to make my visual impairment a whole lot less obvious by already knowing the words. It was a trick I'd mastered in sixth grade. *Memorize everything in advance.* And I was good at it.

As I read the words to one of the last pieces in my folder, I wondered why Choir remained the one holdout for anything "sacred" in the public school system. Why were we still singing about God being a "Mighty Fortress" when we weren't even allowed to pray? Why did high school choirs everywhere still perform sections of the Mass in Latin and Mendelssohn's *Elijah*? I suspected I knew the reason: Students would be robbed of experiencing most of the world's greatest music if sacred pieces were omitted from choir repertoires.

True.

And on any other day, that would have mattered to me. But today I didn't care about experiencing "great" music. All I wanted was to not have to endure some composer's declaration of God's wisdom in creating all things. Even a soppy contemporary love ballad would be preferable to the music I held in my hand.

If there was a God, and if He was so wise, why would He keep creating people with illnesses? With handicaps? With abnormalities? How could anyone who'd taken a serious look at the world really believe that God, reasoning and loving or otherwise—but especially reasoning and loving—was behind it? I didn't want to sing *"Wise and just, creator fair!"* when I felt that there was nothing wise or just or fair about the way I'd been created—and when I didn't even believe that this whole God-thing that my father and even Mr. Parisch seemed to be so confident about was true.

I put away my music.

I could memorize the song later. Perhaps on a day when I didn't feel so resentful. Or . . . maybe I wouldn't memorize it at all. Maybe I'd just drop Choir.

The latter idea gained a whole lot of momentum when I realized who'd just entered the classroom to take the seat beside mine. Dana Cullen.

"Sore tailbone today?" she asked me, giggling.

"No," I told her.

"Nathan told me you're probably legally blind, you know, because you're an albino? Is that true?"

"Yeah."

Then she did it . . . the thing I hated more than any other kind of teasing. She stuck her hand right in my face, held up three fingers, and asked, "How many fingers am I holding up?"

"Three." I glared at her. "Look, everyone. Dana knows how old she is!"

A few kids began to laugh, but a terse sneer from Dana in their direction silenced them. Then she turned back to me. "I bet you think you're so cute, don't you?"

"Actually," I said, "I don't." And that was the end of our conversation.

But the girl sitting in the chair on the other side of me gently tapped my sleeve with the tip of her pencil and asked, "You're not really blind, are you? I mean, I saw you looking at your music."

Her tone seemed genuine enough. It lacked all the sarcasm of Dana's remarks, so I decided to answer her. "I can see. But not as well as you. After a certain point, vision is bad enough that a person can't drive, is eligible for government benefits, and, for all practical purposes according to whoever made the cutoff line, is blind legally. Your vision is 20/20. Mine's 20/400."

"So . . . can you see me?"

"I can see you. But not the details that other people see—like the color of your eyes or the exact expression on your face."

The girl thought about that. "How do you know who people are, then?"

I shrugged. "Well, I knew Dana because of her haircut and the color of her hair. After a while, I'll know everyone in here based on where they sit, or their voices, or the kind of clothes they wear."

"But you might not recognize us if you saw us somewhere else?"

"Right," I said, pleased that I'd finally met another student who was more interested in understanding my disability than in mocking me because of it.

"I'm Katie," she said to me.

I shook her hand when she held it out to me, even though I thought that was a strange thing for a girl to do. "I'm Stephanie. Do you and I share music?" Because the alternative was so unpleasant, I actually prayed while I waited for her to answer. *Please, God, if you're real, let me share music with Katie and not with—*

"No," said Katie. "You share with Dana."

Well, so much for the God theory, I thought.

The choir director arrived, attendance was taken, and we began rehearsal. I stood beside Dana, groping for the second soprano harmony but not for the words. I was sickened to discover that in addition to being an excellent runner, Dana Cullen was a very good singer—a lot better than I'd ever be. She was also thinner and prettier than I'd ever be. And she was the one thing I knew I'd *never* be, at least not here at Canyon Street High—she was popular.

But she's also a snob, I told myself.

Somehow, this failed to console me. I hadn't behaved any more decently toward Dana Cullen than she had behaved toward me. If there was one thing good that I could say about myself, it was that I didn't ridicule people. I knew the pain of being made to feel like slime on the ocean floor. I didn't want my words to cause anyone else to feel that way. Though I had no doubt that my comment to Dana had stolen none of her ample self-esteem, I still regretted saying it.

So after class, I cautiously placed my hand at Dana's elbow as she started to leave the room, and said, "Dana, I'm sorry about what I said earlier. About your being three?"

My expectation was that the average person, in a similar situation, would maybe mutter a *That's okay*, or laugh a little and admit that they had sort of been acting like a three year old.

But apparently, Dana Cullen had a different expectation. Or maybe she just wasn't interested in behaving like the average person. In any case, her response only fueled my determination to beat her in the mile—in front of everyone.

After pulling her arm away from my touch, and staring at me as if I might have just infected her with some dreaded disease, Dana said, "At least *I* know not to try to cross the track when people are running toward me." And then she sauntered away from me and out of the room.

Katie grabbed my arm and, being offended for me said, "Can you believe her?"

I nodded. "I can."

"Well, I can't!" Katie walked out into the hall ahead of me. "As if she's anything so special that she has a right to feel like she's better than everyone else!"

The thing that Katie didn't understand, but Dana Cullen did, is that you didn't have to be anything special to be better than me. You only had to be normal.

Chapter Five

Even though I wasn't hungry, I bought lunch. Then I found an unoccupied table in the cafeteria where I could hopefully sit down in peace and force myself to eat it.

Disgusting-looking, soggy pizza.

The noise of conversation, laughter, the clanging of silverware, and the hum of the tray-return belt surrounded me, but I just stared at the prongs of my fork as I poked at my food, trying to ignore everything and everyone else around me.

What a horrible day it had been. And it was only half over.

Maybe I should have stayed in the dormitory, I thought. Maybe—

"Is it okay if I sit here?"

Startled, I dropped my fork and looked up at the boy who'd just spoken to me. I recognized his voice, and his light blond hair . . . the boy who'd run into me on the track yesterday. The infamous *Nathan* everyone had been feeling sorry for all morning.

"I can't stop you," I said quietly, hoping that he wasn't planning to harass me.

"Well," he said, still standing there holding his tray, "would you if you could? Stop me, I mean. Because I can sit somewhere—"

I smiled. "Just sit down."

He did.

In the chair right beside mine.

"I guess you've been hearing about yesterday all morning," he said. When I didn't answer, he added, "I have."

"Sorry."

He stayed quiet a moment, and then said, "Me too."

We started eating.

"Where'd you move here from?" he ventured after a couple of minutes.

"New England."

"That's got to be a big change." He opened his carton of milk and stuck his straw in. "We moved here last year from Alaska."

I glanced only halfway up at him. "Really?"

"Really."

"Which do you like better?"

He placed his forefinger on the tip of his straw and tapped it a few times. "Here. Definitely here." He began working at his pizza.

I realized something then. Something that embarrassed me a little because it made me feel like a whiner. Yesterday, when I'd assured my father that everyone had laughed at me, pastors' kids and all . . . it had been a lie. True, it had seemed to me at the time that everyone was laughing, but this boy sitting beside me had not laughed. In fact, he had defended me.

And he wasn't laughing now.

"Nathan," I began, but then I stopped. "That's your name, right?"

"Yeah. Nathan Ewen."

"I'm Stephanie Teale," I told him. "Thanks for not laughing at me yesterday."

He shrugged. "Nothing was funny."

"Yeah, well, you're the only one who didn't think so."

"People can be jerks sometimes," he said matter-of-factly. "That's all."

I noticed as we sat there, silent again, that Nathan Ewen was not an unattractive boy. He wasn't tall, but he was fit. His haircut was stylish and neat. And he had dark eyes; I couldn't tell the color, exactly, except that they were too dark to be blue. A good-looking guy had never before joined me for lunch, and I began to feel nervous. So much for eating my pizza!

When Nathan finished his food, he slid his tray forward a bit and turned in his chair to look straight at me. "Do you have any plans for after high school?" he asked.

"Not really," I admitted. "You?"

He nodded. "I'm training to be a paramedic."

"Really?"

"Yeah. They've started up this program for teenagers where we take classes. Eventually we'll get to ride along and then actually assist on emergency calls."

"Wow! Have you gone on any calls yet?"

"No. Not yet. Next month."

"You are the first person I've met who really seems to know what you want to do," I said.

"I didn't always know," he said. "See, last summer, my brother drowned. I knew CPR, and I was doing it, but it wasn't helping. Nothing was helping. He was just . . . *dead*."

He went quiet, and I looked down at my plate. "How horrible. I'm sorry, Nathan."

"No," he said. "We kept doing it and finally got his pulse. I remember thinking, when the paramedics got there, that this was what I wanted to do. I wanted to know what to do when someone needed help. I wanted to know how to do it. And I wanted to be there to do it." He shrugged. "So that's what I'm doing."

"So . . . how's your brother?" I asked cautiously. "Is he okay, and everything?"

He laughed. "He's fine."

"Good."

"*He* wants to be a preacher in some remote jungle somewhere," Nathan said, respect for his brother evident in every word of the statement. "I'll have to introduce him to you sometime. He's a senior." He grinned. "You haven't told me what you'd like to do."

I looked away from him again. I had always been reluctant to think too much about what I might like to do with my life. Who was going to hire me, anyway? My parents wanted me to go to college, and that's probably what I'd end up doing, but I felt no great yearning toward any specific career.

So many things I might have been interested in pursuing had already been eliminated for me because of my visual impairment. Like many kids, I'd grown up wanting to be an astronaut, but an astronaut has to have perfect vision.

Then I'd considered a career in computers. Even though computer technology could be adapted to a visually impaired user, the reality of spending eight or ten hours a day in a situation where my life was directed by what I could see on a screen in front of me . . . it just wasn't practical.

I loved to act, and I knew that I could be great at it, but, really now . . . how many roles are there for the average everyday albino? Not many. And even if there were, I'd have to get through an audition. I'd tried that once already, and it had been totally humiliating. Trying to "act" while holding a poorly made copy of the script as far away from my face as I could get it and still read it—a disaster, plain and simple.

I knew there were plenty of things I could do, but none of them seemed to intrigue me as much as the things I knew I couldn't do. For example, a career in medicine. How exciting. How rewarding. How . . . significant.

I placed my fork beside my plate and moved my tray aside. "I don't really know, Nathan. I wish I could do something like what you're doing, but there's just no way."

Nathan thought for a long moment before responding. When he did, his tone was quiet and sincere. "It's true that there are a lot of things you have to be able to see. All the minute measurements of medications, all the equipment. But you could learn first aid, Stephanie. You could do CPR." He stared right at me. "You could save someone's life."

He paused. "Anyway, you might not like being a paramedic. Everyone's different, with different gifts and talents. The trick is to figure out what *yours* are and find something to do that uses them."

I didn't get an opportunity to comment—which was probably a good thing since I had no idea what I would have said—because several girls helped themselves to the rest of the chairs at the table, set their trays down, and started talking to Nathan . . . about me, as if I wasn't even there.

"Why are you eating over here with *her?*"

"Did you hear about what she said to Dana in Choir?"

"I actually think her hair's kind of pretty, but . . . it's white as snow!"

I grabbed my tray and stood to leave, but Nathan placed his hand on my arm and said, "Wait. I'll introduce you." After telling me the name of each girl present, and telling them mine—twice, and loudly, taking care to enunciate every syllable for them—he moved his hand away from my arm and joined me standing. "I'll walk with you to your next class."

"You don't have to do that," I said. "I think I know the way."

He grinned. "I didn't think you didn't."

I shrugged—my way of giving him permission if that's what he really wanted to do. "Okay."

Nathan Ewen and I left the cafeteria together then, and I would have given anything to see—to really see—the expressions on those girls' faces because they'd suddenly gone completely speechless.

Chapter Six

"I want all the milers at the gate," the coach announced. "We're going to do a distance workout today."

I didn't know what that meant, exactly, since this was my first time at an actual track practice. But I had my suspicions. And the moaning and groaning of the other mile runners—six boys and the five girls I'd run against yesterday—confirmed them.

We were going to hit the streets.

"Six miles today," the coach said as he jogged past us at a fairly strenuous pace. "You know the route. We're a group today. No sprinting. No walking. Let's go!"

Six miles. That would be easy enough. Since the group had to stay together, I wouldn't have to worry about getting lost. Dana Cullen and I would not be competing, and neither she nor anyone else would be stupid enough to waste any breath harassing me. So all I had to do was run. Unwind. Relax.

And watch my step so that I didn't trip over a curb and fall on my face in front of these people too!

We ran along one residential street until it ended at a huge empty field, and then we turned west on a dirt trail. Most of the boys and the coach had gotten a little ahead of us girls, but I didn't mind. As long as I could always see one person ahead of me, I'd know where to go. The trail was narrow and not quite level, but the area was so beautiful that I didn't mind the extra challenge. The smell of new grass, still moist from a recent rain, and the rise of the mountains against the sky further west, captivated my imagination. Sure, there were mountains in New England, but they were weathered and rounded, tree-covered to the top. Here in Colorado, the mountains were rocky and impetuous. Untamed. Pristine. I'd visited them many times with my father and couldn't wait to return.

If there was one place on this earth where I could seriously consider the possibility of the existence of God, it was in the mountains. Rugged, yet beautiful. Always changing, yet immovable. A splendor standing in complete indifference to humanity. Whenever I tried to push my way up the slope of a peak in spite of a driving wind that seemed to want me to stay back, or when I stood on a boulder unable to hear my own thoughts because of the roaring of the river below me, or when a huge thunderstorm crowded the top of the mountain with its noise and hail and power, the sense of my own smallness always reminded me that if there was a center to this universe, it certainly wasn't *me*. And at those moments, the idea of the earth just randomly coming into existence never seemed to be able to persuade me the way it could in a classroom.

Something had to have created this, I'd think. Something brilliant. Something huge.

But down here in the real world that made up ninety-nine percent of my life, I just couldn't be so sure.

"Stephanie, watch your step!"

A hand from somewhere behind me grabbed my elbow, but not before the toe of my shoe caught the bottom side of a root and held there, even as the rest of me kept moving forward. I managed to yank it loose before falling flat on my face, but I had to come down hard on my other foot to catch myself.

Too hard.

I felt my ankle twist underneath me. Tears filled my eyes before I even realized they were coming, and I moved quickly off the trail to determine if I'd really hurt myself or if it was just going to feel that way for a couple of minutes.

The girl who'd grabbed my arm let go of it. "Are you okay?"

After taking several steps in the grass beside the trail, I nodded. "I can walk on it . . . but it does hurt. I don't think I'd better finish running."

"I'll run ahead and tell Coach," she said.

A voice behind me said, "While you're at it, Brit, tell him I'm walking her back to the school."

The girl squinted at me for a moment before nodding quickly and stepping back onto the trail.

I waited for Brit to get several feet away from me before I spoke to the boy behind me. I didn't have to turn to face him, so I didn't. I recognized his voice. I knew who he was. And I didn't want his help, even though I'd definitely enjoyed it earlier in the cafeteria. "Nathan," I said, "I can get back on my own."

"Oh, don't tell me that," he said. "I've got this sideache you wouldn't believe, and you're the only excuse I'm going to get to quit running."

I couldn't help smiling, though I tried not to let it show too much when I finally did turn to look at Nathan. "You could always do something crazy like tell the coach you have a sideache," I suggested.

"Nah," he said. "That would ruin my image. Nathan Ewen, CSH's best miler, doesn't stop for sideaches." He laughed quietly, then, after pulling in a deep breath and pressing his hand against his side, he sat on a fallen log. "Have a seat for a minute, Stephanie. Let me take a look at your ankle."

I sat beside him, but I didn't take him up on his offer to examine my foot. At least I knew he wasn't lying to me about having a sideache. But what was he doing? Why was he being so nice to me? Most guys would probably rather run ten miles, sideache or not, than be seen with someone like me.

After giving Nathan several minutes to catch his breath, I grinned. "Okay," I said. "I think my ankle's feeling strong enough to head back now. Thanks for waiting for me."

He laughed as he got up and held his hand out to help me do the same. "Yeah. Sure."

We started walking silently back the way we had come.

Since I thought I'd heard a hint of irritation in his tone, and since it had not been my intention to embarrass him—I had yet to meet a runner who didn't know all too much about sideaches—I said, "My former coach always told me that I wouldn't get painful sideaches so frequently if I breathed in through my nose and out through my mouth when I run."

"Yeah, I know that," he said, sounding a little defensive.

I sighed. The male ego could be such a nuisance sometimes. "Well, they happen to all of us." Then I hurried to change the subject. "Do you ever get out to the mountains?"

"Sure." His tone sounded relaxed again. "In fact, my brother and I are going to head up there for some four-wheel driving in a couple of weeks."

"Sounds fun," I said.

"It is. Some of those old mining and logging roads are pretty rugged."

"What kind of car have you got?" I asked, trying to sound interested. Guys who liked to drive around old logging roads usually liked to talk about their trucks.

"My brother's got the four-wheel drive," he said. "A Jeep."

That's it? I thought when he didn't say anything more. I'd anticipated hearing about lift-kits, oversized tires, fog lights, and roll bars all the way back to the school. Of course, it was his brother's 4×4 and not his own.

"I like the mountains," he said quietly. "They're a good reminder of how small we are and how big God is."

Strange, the way he'd so casually chosen a route for our conversation that came so close to my own thoughts a few minutes back. I wondered if his statement reflected some kind of belief in

God, or if, like me, he just couldn't escape feeling that way in the mountains.

I wondered, but I didn't ask. Hearing about lift-kits and tires all the way back to the school was one thing. Hearing about God for that long was something else. "Do you ski?" I asked him.

"I have," he said. "But it's not one of my favorite things to do. You?"

"Cross-country. Downhill's just a little too scary for me."

He nodded. "I guess it would be when you can't see rocks and—sorry."

"That's okay," I told him. "And actually, it's the cliffs I tend to worry about not seeing till it's too late."

He laughed. "No doubt."

"I know people with worse vision than mine who actually downhill ski, but I guess I'm just not that adventurous."

"Cross-country's better exercise anyway," Nathan said.

"Exactly."

By this time, we'd reached the start of the dirt trail and had stepped off it onto pavement again.

"How's the ankle?" Nathan wanted to know.

"It's okay."

He grinned. "Liar."

"It's stiffening up pretty good," I admitted. "But I'll get some ice on it when I get home, and it'll be okay."

"Good thing there's no meet this weekend."

I nodded. "When is the first one?"

"Next Saturday."

Eight days. My ankle should be healed by then. I should be able to compete. But without the opportunity to train early in the week, I had to wonder whether I'd be much of a factor in the race.

And Dana Cullen? It looked like I wouldn't be finishing ahead of her anytime soon.

But I could wait.

The more difficult the task, the sweeter the accomplishment.

And when I stepped across the finish line with Dana Cullen behind me—with everyone there to see it—it was going to be sweet indeed.

"Do you have a car at school," Nathan asked, "or will you have to call someone to pick you up?"

"I usually walk, but I'm sure my mother will come get me today." I looked at Nathan and smiled. "I don't drive."

He stopped walking to stare up at the sky and shake his head. "I'm so stupid. I'm sorry, Stephanie. I mean, I know you're legally blind, but I guess I forgot because you don't *seem* . . . well, you get around without help and . . ." He shook his head again. "I'm just sticking my foot further down my throat, aren't I?"

"Nathan," I said, "I don't necessarily want the fact that I'm legally blind being foremost in people's minds when they think about me. I just want them to think of me as a person. So, actually, your forgetting that I can't drive is kind of like a compliment—in its own weird way. It means that you forgot for a minute that I can't see that well and were just thinking of me as Stephanie." I smiled. "So don't worry about it. Okay?"

"Okay," he said. "But if I ever forget when you don't want me to . . . you know, if you need help with something, don't be afraid to remind me."

I nodded. I could live with that.

"And," he said, "I can give you a ride home so your mom doesn't have to pick you up . . . if you want."

Again, I nodded.

I could live with that too.

Chapter Seven

"There. How's that?" My mother had just finished piling pillows onto the coffee table, sitting me down on the couch and propping my foot up, putting an ice pack on my ankle, covering me with an afghan, and plopping a huge bowl of buttered popcorn in my lap. "Are you all right?"

I laughed. "Yes, Ma. It's only a twisted ankle. Probably not even sprained. You're acting like I broke it or something."

"It's just that I know how important your running is to you," she said. She sat beside me and grabbed a handful of popcorn. "I want you healed up as soon as possible."

"Me too."

"So tell me, Stephanie; who brought you home?"

"Oh, this guy . . ."

Ma elbowed me. "See? Didn't I tell you you'd make friends?"

"He was just being nice."

"And what do you think friendship is if it doesn't start with being nice?"

Why couldn't my mother ever just leave me alone? "People are nice for all kinds of reasons, Ma. Friendship doesn't necessarily have to have anything to do with it." I shoved a few pieces of popcorn into my mouth. "I think Nathan's being nice to me because he feels bad about running into me on the track, that's all." I shrugged. "He's planning to be a paramedic. Maybe he's just interested in me scientifically . . . you know—"

"Interested in you scientifically?" Ma shook her head. "Stephanie, I honestly don't understand you sometimes! Why *wouldn't* someone like you? Aside from being cynical about everyone's motives, you're lots of fun to be around. You—"

"What do you mean by that?"

Ma sighed. So did I. Here we go again.

"I mean," Ma said, "the fact that the thought would even cross your mind that this boy is interested in you scientifically is ridiculous! I know that you're different. I know how cruel kids are. I know it's hard for you. But why is it so impossible for you to believe that someone would like you just for *you?* If people are nice to you, you automatically assume it's because they feel sorry for you, or because it makes them feel better about themselves that they were nice to the poor little albino, and now . . . because he's interested in you scientifically!"

I had to laugh. It *was* kind of ridiculous. "Okay, okay, Ma. Calm down. You're right about that one. I concede!"

"It's not enough for you to concede, honey," she insisted. "You have to *believe* me."

"Yeah, well, that's easier said than done."

Ma let out a long breath, and she looked away from me toward Shakespeare's cage. "There are always going to be people who won't accept you, Stephanie," she said softly. "Even when you're an adult living in the supposedly adult world. People who'll think you're too 'handicapped' to baby-sit their kids, or too different to be part of their circle of friends, or too much of a risk to hire on. But if you accept yourself, it won't be able to hurt you the way it does now because you'll know that *they're* the ones with the problem and not you."

"Ma," I said as gently as I could, "in case you haven't looked at me lately, I *am* the one with the problem. I am different."

I knew before she even opened her mouth that she was about to launch into her *Everybody's Different in Their Own Way* lecture, and I didn't want to hear it. There was a big difference between being different because you chose to wear plaid pants with a striped shirt and being different genetically. But I sat still while my mother talked because I knew that trying to help me helped her. When she finished, I said, "I think it's going to be the rare person who can really accept me."

"Maybe so," Ma said. "But why can't you look at a person who *is* nice to you as one of those 'rare' people right from the start instead of always believing that there has to be some shrouded motive?"

"I don't know."

Actually, I did know. I just didn't want to talk about it with my mother. If I allowed myself to believe that . . . Nathan, say . . . was one of those rare people who could really accept me, and then found out later that he was only being nice to me because he felt sorry for me . . . ? I had to protect myself from that.

Ma cleared her throat. "Stephanie, you are—"

I ate popcorn and ignored her next litany of words. The *You Are a Wonderful, Witty, Smart, Talented, and Beautiful Person* lecture was as familiar as the blinking cursor on the computer screen when you can't think of a way to start that dreaded English assignment. As familiar, and as annoying.

But the last thing she said before getting up to prepare dinner penetrated the solid wall of my determination not to hear her. It was something she'd never added onto the lecture before. Something I'd never even considered.

"Stephanie, if you make it so impossible for people to earn friendship from you, you're going to drive them away. Not your white hair. Not your poor eyesight. *You.*"

I stayed on the couch, eating way too much popcorn, unable to dismiss those words—and their probable and frightening truth—from my mind. It was certainly convenient for me to say that so-and-so didn't want to hang around with me because I'm an albino. But what if all those so-and-so's had simply wearied of my cold and skeptical response to their attempts at friendship? Had I walled myself so solidly inside my own understanding of "the way kids are" that I wouldn't know a true friend if he or she was right there in front of me?

Maybe.

But . . . maybe not.

I didn't know.

I did know that if Nathan Ewen, or Katie, or anyone else at Canyon Street High really *did* want to be my friend, I didn't want to drive them away.

I'd have to take a chance. I'd have to make myself accept that Nathan Ewen was being nice to me because . . . because he was a nice person, and that's all. And if it turned out that he did have some other reason . . .? Well, at least I'd have given him a chance.

I'd spent so much of my life lamenting the fact—or what I thought was the fact—that people never gave me a chance . . . and here I was, possibly guilty of the very same thing!

Well, not anymore. Not here.

I'd have to learn to make friends among "normal" people sooner or later, or else be friendless, because my safe place, the school for the blind, was now two-thirds of a continent away.

I set the bowl of popcorn on the coffee table. "What's for dinner?" I asked my mother.

"Chicken." She came into the living room again to sit beside me. As she dried her hands on a dishtowel, she said, "Stephanie, your father asked me something this morning that I want to talk to you about before he gets home."

"Well, you better talk fast then," I said. It was almost that time already.

Ma nodded. "He asked me if I'd like to go to church with him Sunday, and if I thought you might like to."

"What did you tell him?" I asked cautiously.

"I told him I'd go . . . and that I didn't think you'd want to."

"Good," I said, relieved. "You don't really believe all that God-stuff, do you, Ma?"

She didn't answer right away, as I thought she would.

"Ma?"

"No . . . well, I don't know, Stephanie. I'd like to, I guess. And it's just too much to believe that your father could change himself as much as he's changed, *by himself.*" She laughed. "That didn't make any sense, did it?"

It made more sense than I cared to admit.

"He explained it to me like this," Ma said. "He'd spent his life looking for things to make him happy and give him purpose. He did sports. He worked so he could make a lot of money. He married me. We had you." She paused. "All of these things were supposed to fill him up inside, but they only did for a little while, and then that meaninglessness would be there again. Not because he didn't love me or you, or because he didn't get any satisfaction out of his work. He did. It's just, he said, there was always an emptiness way down inside. Like life's a huge field of stuff that we can sort through to try to keep ahead of feeling like we really have nothing."

"How depressing," I said, even though I'd experienced exactly what Ma was talking about. Winning medals, getting that new blouse, upgrading to that faster computer, receiving a wave in the hall from that guy you thought would never acknowledge your existence . . . they all felt great at first, but eventually and always I'd ended up needing to win the next race, tired of that old new blouse, wanting the newest thing in computer technology, and upset because the wave from the boy hadn't led to actual conversation. Eventually and always, I'd run out of that satisfied *Okay, life is good now* feeling.

"Then someone told your father about Jesus," Ma continued. "He read something to me out of the Bible about a man finding a hidden treasure in a field and was so happy about it that he sold everything else he owned so he could buy that field."

I held up my hand. "You're losing me, Ma."

She smiled. "Sorry. He said that finding out about God and His plan for his life was like finding the hidden treasure in the huge field of stuff he'd already been digging through. But unlike all the other stuff, the treasure doesn't lose its value, or its newness, or its meaning." Ma looked down at her knees. "I guess I'm tired of just sorting through stuff when I could be digging for treasure."

"Ma," I said, "this is way too deep for me. Right now, my goal in life is to figure out how to survive the rest of the school year with my ego intact. That's reality. And it's very daily and takes all my energy. I don't have time to be philosophical."

"Well," she said, "will you think about coming to church with us?" She stood and went back to the kitchen. "An hour and a half on a Sunday morning isn't that big a deal, is it? Even if it ends up meaning nothing to you, I know it would mean a lot to your dad."

"I'll think about it," I grudgingly promised.

Chapter Eight

I woke up early Sunday morning. Before my alarm. Before sunrise. I hadn't had a bad dream. My ankle wasn't hurting. I didn't know why I was awake—but I knew that trying to go back to sleep would be a waste of time. I had always been one of those people who needed two or three hours to shut down the thinking process at night before I could fall asleep and then woke up in the morning with my mind already in full gear. So I lay there under my blankets, staring at the gray half-light outside my curtains, doing exactly what I didn't want to be doing.

Thinking.

I'd had little peace after my mother's comment about driving potential friends away, and even less after I'd imperiously announced to my father that I had no intention of going to church with him. He had quietly and calmly accepted my decision and had immediately moved the conversation in another direction, but I hadn't missed his disappointment . . . or my mother's.

I didn't want to disappoint my parents . . . especially not when it could be avoided by something as effortless on my part as enduring a church service.

What could it hurt? Really.

So I'd get a little bored . . . and maybe a little irritated. So what?

My father could have easily chosen the route of "As long as you live under my roof . . . " But he hadn't. He could have spent every meal he and Ma and I shared together spouting off about God . . . but he hadn't. He was clearly willing to give me some room, time, and respect. Maybe this was one way I could return the favor.

I'd go today. If I liked it, great. Maybe I'd think about going again. If I didn't like it? Well, at least he'd know I'd been willing to give it a try.

Ma and Dad were downstairs already by the time I walked into the kitchen for breakfast. "Will this be okay?" I asked them, turning in the doorway for them to evaluate the skirt and sweater I had finally chosen to wear. I'd never gone to church before. Except for what I'd seen on television, I had no idea how one was expected to dress.

"It's fine," Dad said, standing to hug me. "Beautiful. But I thought you—"

I pulled away from him and reached to open the cupboard to get myself a glass. "I changed my mind."

"I'm glad," he said, and then asked me whether I'd prefer pancakes or waffles.

We agreed on waffles, and then, before I knew it—too quickly, it seemed—we were getting out of the car in the parking lot at Dad's church. The building in front of me was large, brick, with an intimidating flight of cement steps leading to the door. The name of the church as well as a few other things appeared on a sign at the edge of the lawn, but I was too far away from it to read what it said. The parking lot itself was noisy with cars pulling in, doors shutting, and conversation. Smiles. Dresses. Suit coats. Bibles.

My stomach tightened.

"Come on," Dad urged Ma and me. "I'll find the pastor and introduce you."

I almost groaned aloud. But the dreaded moment was deferred, at least for a few minutes, by someone who stopped Dad in the parking lot to talk with him.

I stayed slightly behind Dad, nervously kicking at the gravel at my feet. Suddenly I remembered Mr. Parisch's remark about parking lot gravel . . . that I'd never looked closely at it . . . which, of course, I hadn't. I'd assumed at the time that he was trying to tell me that parking lot rocks (and me, since I'd made the comparison) were beautiful too, even if in a different way than rubies in a treasure chest.

A sentiment I didn't share.

Still, as I stood there, no longer kicking the rocks, I couldn't help wondering what a parking lot rock *did* look like close up. It could never be beautiful, could it? A chunk of gravel?

Quickly, when I thought that nobody would notice, I bent and chose a piece at random. At first, it looked exactly as parking lot rocks always looked. Small. White. Uninteresting. Not ugly, maybe, but certainly not beautiful. But as I brought it closer to my eyes and turned it in my fingers, I noticed narrow stripes of pale blue. And then some mauve. Then I noticed its shape . . . and its texture. It wasn't uninteresting at all.

Dad's hand on my shoulder startled me. Laughing nervously, I dropped the rock and muttered something about the bother of walking through gravel in sandals.

I followed my parents up the steps—I counted nine—and inside. The auditorium or meeting hall or whatever you called it was simple enough. Chairs. A piano. A pulpit. A cross on the wall. Blue. Several people greeted Dad and then stared at me while introductions were made.

"Good to have you!"

"Glad you could be here today!"

"Praise God!"

"You have the most beautiful hair, young lady!"

Please.

"The restrooms are right down the hall."

"Thank you," I said to the older man who'd uttered that—the only useful statement I'd heard so far.

Dad located the pastor and his wife, introduced them to Ma and me by their first names—which unnerved me—and then we found some chairs a few rows back from the front.

"Can you see okay from here, Stephanie?" Dad asked. "We can move closer if——"

"No. This is okay." I doubted there'd be all that much to see, anyway. Some guy talking. I wondered if Dad's pastor was the type to wave his Bible around in the air.

"Your pastor and his wife seem really nice," Ma said to Dad.

Dad nodded. "I wouldn't be where I am right now if . . . "

I turned away from my parents when someone sat beside me and started talking to me. I looked intently at the boy, trying to determine whether or not I knew him. Blond hair. It could be Nathan Ewen, but I couldn't be sure.

"When you told me your last name," he said, "it didn't even click in my mind that you could be Dr. Teale's daughter."

Finally recognizing his voice enough to be certain that this *was* Nathan, I smiled and asked, "What are you doing here?" Then I chided myself. That was a stupid thing to say. "Never mind," I said to him. "Don't answer that. Obviously, you're here for church."

He smiled. "Obviously." After speaking briefly with my father about track and then about some new study Bible, Nathan turned back to me. "You look nice." He fidgeted nervously. "I mean, I'm used to seeing you in sweats."

"Thanks," I said quietly, embarrassed. Then, noting his brightly patterned tie and crisp black dress shirt, I added, "So do you."

"How's your ankle?"

"It's still a little sore, but it's a lot better."

"Good." We sat for a moment or two, neither of us knowing what to say, and then Nathan stood. "Do you want to come meet some of our youth group kids?"

I didn't, but I said, "Sure."

After meeting several kids whose names I'd probably never remember—Tony, Natalie, Josh, Coreen—I followed Nathan out into the hallway where he introduced me to his brother, Judah, and a girl named Rebekah.

Judah held out his hand to me. "Hi, Stephanie."

"Hi." I noticed his firm grip as I briefly shook his hand and then hurried to let it go to grab Rebekah's outstretched hand. Another strong handshake.

"That's a gorgeous sweater," she complimented me. "The color looks great on you."

That was one thing I never had to worry about—my skin tone clashing with autumn colors . . . or winter colors, pastels, primary colors, warm colors, cool colors, earth tones. White pretty much worked with everything!

"Thank you," I said to Rebekah.

"Stephanie runs the mile too," Nathan told her. He seemed almost proud of the fact.

"I'd die if I even tried it," Rebekah said.

Music started in the auditorium then, and Nathan suggested that we'd better go find our seats. But before we did, Rebekah said, "It was nice to meet you, Stephanie."

I nodded. *Yeah, right. You're just being polite because we're in church.* Then I remembered what my mother had said. "Thanks," I said. "It was good to meet you too."

Nathan and I walked back together to where my parents were sitting, and then he left quickly to find his mother.

I stood with everyone in the place—about three hundred people, it seemed to me. I didn't know the hymn they were singing, so I just listened, and was somewhat surprised to discover that even though the words were old, full of *thee's, thou's, thy's,* and *trusteth's,* the people around me were singing them as if they knew exactly what they meant and really believed them for their lives right now. When the music stopped, someone stepped up to give a few announcements and welcome visitors before the pastor went to the pulpit and started his speech.

I tried to make myself comfortable in the cold metal folding chair. "I got a letter from my daughter this week," the pastor began. "She's away at Bible college, some of you know, and it seems this year she's been getting her first real taste of some of the differences we Christians have with one another. Interpretation differences. Character differences. Life philosophy differences. I got to thinking about this as I prayed about writing her a letter back that would be helpful, and I decided that maybe it would be beneficial for all of us to have a brief reminder of where we're the same." He paused. "Let's pray."

I bowed my head, thinking that—if nothing else—I would get a good idea of what my father had gotten himself into.

After an enthusiastic *amen* from the congregation, the pastor started talking again. "Look around you," he said. "No two people in this building are exactly alike. Even the Benantis' little twins have their own personalities. We as people are different."

Oh no, I thought, here it comes. Did my father set this up? Because if he did . . .

"Some of us are tall, some are short," the pastor continued. "Some of us are thin, some of us—" he paused to pat his stomach—"are not as thin."

People chuckled, but I didn't see why. It wasn't as if the man was huge.

"Some of us have blond hair," he went on, "red hair, brown hair, black hair, gray hair, white hair, no hair."

More laughter.

"We come from different ethnic backgrounds. Different races. Our personalities are different. Some of us are aggressive;

some are passive. Some people anger easily; some don't. Some of us are confident in who we are; many are not. Some make a lot of money; most don't."

More laughter . . . but quieter.

"I could go on all day naming all the ways in which we, as human beings, differ. But there's one way in which we're all the same." He opened his Bible. The auditorium was silent except for the rustle of pages being turned. Thin pages. "*Romans 3:23. For all have sinned, and come short of the glory of God,*" he read.

Then he spent several minutes reading other passages from the Bible that said basically the same thing. Finally, he closed the Book, leaned forward on the podium, and said, "We are all sinners. Every one of us."

Why hadn't I guessed that he was going to say that? Didn't preachers always say that sooner or later? I'd spent many hours longing to be the same as everyone else. I didn't want to finally be told that I *was*—if it was only because I'm a sinner and so are they!

"I think very few people would dispute the fact that we all do wrong," the pastor explained. "We might have different definitions of what right and wrong are, but I doubt that anyone would have the nerve to say that he's lived perfectly, even according to his own standards of right and wrong."

That was true, I had to agree. Nobody was perfect—whatever "perfect" might be.

"And how many of us, even if we know exactly what is right and wrong, still do wrong sometimes?"

Several people in the crowd muttered acknowledgment that they did.

"We all sin. That is one thing that has remained constant throughout all generations of humanity."

I stiffened in my chair and braced myself.

"But there's good news," the pastor said. He opened his Bible again. "Isaiah 53:6," he said when he'd found the page he wanted.

SNOW

"All we like sheep have gone astray; we have turned every one to his own way; and the Lord hath laid on him the iniquity of us all."

I decided I'd better pay attention. I'd never heard anything like that before.

"All kinds of people spend all kinds of time trying to deny their sin, or trying to hide it, or trying to find a way to make themselves acceptable to God in spite of it. Some people even try to reimagine God so that He doesn't require perfection. There are all kinds of things we do to try to come to terms with our own sinfulness—and the resulting lack of peace inside ourselves. We blame it on others. We justify it, or we ignore it, or maybe we call it something else. The concept of *wrong* is rapidly disappearing from our values as a nation. But it has never disappeared from God's. And it never will. That's why each of us—and here's another place where we're the same—needs a Savior. We all need a way to be cleansed of our sinfulness so that we can be reconciled to God. And there is only one way."

I leaned slightly forward in my chair. If this was true, and you could know what that one way was, wouldn't it be exactly like finding a hidden treasure? *The* hidden treasure of the universe? The one that Ma had been rambling on about the other night? Real life stuff . . . not just philosophy?

It had been exactly that for my father.

The pastor read more passages from his Bible. Passages about Jesus. About His crucifixion and resurrection. Passages about forgiveness. Passages about faith. He concluded with something else out of the book of Isaiah.

" . . . *though your sins be as scarlet, they shall be as white as snow . . .* "

He continued speaking after that—about his daughter's dilemma and unity among Christians—but I couldn't stop thinking about the things he'd read from his Bible. *If* there really was a God, and if He did require perfection as the Bible seemed to suggest, and if He really had sent His Son to die to purchase whoever among mankind would believe in Him . . . that would include me, wouldn't it, if I decided that I could overlook all my doubts and believe? Even though people had never accepted me, I could know that God did?

No. It was too simple. Too much to hope for.

I sat through the rest of the service, captivated by the pastor's convictions, but still unsure enough of everything to simply accept him at his word. I knew that *he* believed what he was saying. The question was . . . could I?

I'd have to give it some time, I decided. Maybe I'd talk with my father. Maybe I'd talk with Nathan. Maybe I could go home after church and forget about it. That's what I most wanted to do. But I had a clawing feeling in my stomach that told me it wasn't going to be easy.

After a final prayer and another hymn that I didn't know, I followed my parents back to the entryway. We were stopped there by the pastor and his wife with an invitation to lunch at their house.

Dad and Ma accepted immediately, and I shuddered inside. No matter how nice or how genuine Dad's pastor seemed to be, he was still a pastor, and the last thing I wanted to do was be a guest in his home.

But then Nathan stepped up beside him and said, "Good job today, Dad."

While my parents and several other people nearby enthusiastically agreed, I folded my arms across my chest and tried to keep my face expressionless. Nathan . . . a pastor's kid?

Chapter Nine

"These are Italian tacos," Mrs. Ewen told Ma, Dad, and me as she sat beside her husband at their dining room table. "They're kind of an invention of Ben's."

Tomato sauce, mushrooms, chopped black olives, hamburger, pepperoni, sour cream, and mozzarella cheese all burritoed in a soft flour tortilla. It looked and smelled delicious, and I couldn't wait to taste it.

"Let's pray," said Pastor Ewen. "Nathan?"

I pulled my hand quickly away from my food.

Nathan bowed his head. "Lord, thank You for this food and for this time with the Teales." He paused as if he might be thinking of saying something more but then said only, "Amen."

"Amen." We started eating.

The Italian tacos were delicious.

"Where's your brother?" I whispered to Nathan.

He grinned. "Having lunch with Rebekah and her family."

"Ah." Nathan's smile made me wonder whether there might be just a little more in that information than what he'd actually spoken. I decided not to speculate.

After some conversation with my parents, Pastor Ewen turned to me and asked, "How do you like Canyon Street High, Stephanie?"

I shrugged. "It's school."

"Nathan says some of the kids are pretty hard on you."

I glanced coldly toward Nathan, not sure whether to feel angry or flattered that he'd been talking about me. Turning back to his father, I said, "I *am* somewhat of an oddity."

Pastor Ewen chuckled. "There are worse ways to be odd, believe me."

I laughed. I could think of a few examples of that myself. Like the girl at the school for the blind who got a kick out of putting her glass eyes where she knew they'd make people scream when they found them. *That* was odd.

"I think your hair's beautiful," said Mrs. Ewen.

I could tell by her tone that she wasn't just saying that to be nice. So I said, "Thank you."

"You should see it in a French braid," Nathan said. His father stopped with his taco halfway to his mouth to stare curiously at him, and Nathan quickly helped himself to a second taco.

I hurried to change the subject. "Our first track meet is coming up." I knew the comment would seem random and misplaced to everyone at the table, but anything was better than talking about my hair.

"Yes," said Pastor Ewen. "We'll be there."

I glanced at my parents. Would they be there? I hadn't thought to ask them until now.

"So will we," Dad promised.

"Stephanie's an excellent runner," Nathan said.

Again, I glanced at him, puzzled—and a little embarrassed.

After taking a slow sip of her soda, Mrs. Ewen asked, "Can I ask you something, Stephanie?"

"Sure."

"What . . . what can you see?"

"Mom!"

I had to smile at Nathan's tone. After assuring him that I wasn't offended, I did my best to explain my limitations to Pastor and Mrs. Ewen. But this was never an easy task. Since I had never experienced what it was like to see normally, it was difficult to answer questions like: Is everything blurry to you? Do things just sort of blend together? So, are you more nearsighted or farsighted? Can you see colors the same way we do? But I could give an example. "Look at the tree outside the window," I said.

Everyone at the table did.

"What do you see?"

"Leaves budding," said Mrs. Ewen.

"Shadows," Nathan said.

"Can you see the pattern of the bark?" I asked.

"Mm-hmm," Pastor Ewen answered.

"What about the leaves?" I said. "Can you see them individually?"

Dad said, "Yeah."

"What I see," I said, "is a trunk that looks kind of brown, kind of gray. I see green on the branches, and I know they're leaves, but I couldn't tell you whether they were oak or maple, small or large. I wouldn't see fruit unless it was a really bright color, and I never see birds." I smiled. "But I hear them."

"School must be very difficult for you," Pastor Ewen said quietly.

"Actually, I've figured out ways around most of the visual things." I looked down at my unfinished meal. "It's looking so different that makes school difficult."

"How do you take notes?" Nathan asked. "All my teachers write stuff on the board or on an overhead projector."

"They also lecture," I pointed out. "I write down everything they say while they're writing on the board or overhead. I take a lot more notes than the average person that way, but it pays off at exam time."

"What about math?" he asked.

"That's a little harder," I admitted. "I usually have to go in after class and get the teacher to demonstrate how to work an equation on a sheet of paper for me."

"Do they usually cooperate?"

"Usually." I laughed. "Some of them resent the extra work, or they might be of the opinion that everyone with any 'special needs' should be in Special Ed. all the time, but they'll almost always decide to help after I start going on about my rights to a free and equal education and all that." I paused. "The only class that is really a pain is P.E."

"Really?" Nathan sounded surprised.

"Well, think about it," I urged him. "How many activities in P.E. have something to do with a ball, or a birdie, or whatever?"

"I wouldn't have thought of that," he admitted.

"I'm always the last person chosen when we have to choose up teams—and I can't even blame the other kids for that. I *hate* P.E. Talk about feeling like an absolute loser!"

"But you're such a good athlete."

I smiled at him. "You just haven't seen me on a tennis court . . . or a basketball court . . . baseball diamond . . . soccer field. You name it, I'm no good at it!"

"Well," Ma said, "you're a great runner."

"And she's not a bad swimmer, either," Dad added.

"Okay," I said, embarrassed again. "Can we talk about someone else now?"

"Stephanie," Pastor Ewen said, "I want you to know one thing before we do that. The Bible says that God knows us from the time we're in our mother's womb. It says that He forms us there. He didn't overlook you. He didn't make a mistake. Yes, you're different. We live in a fallen world where there are diseases, handicaps, and genetic abnormalities. But that doesn't mean that any of them are random or somehow unnoticed by

God. You are the way you are just like I'm the way I am . . . and God loves you the way you are. He can use you the way you are. And He can give you peace, even joy, about the way you are."

Nobody spoke for what seemed like several minutes. Finally, I said, "You're a pastor. You have to say that."

"That's not true," he said. "I knew a man with cerebral palsy who visited a church where the pastor told him he was that way because he was a child of the devil."

"I would never go to church again," I said.

"And he didn't. Not for a long time. But see, I don't *have* to say God loves you the way you are. I say it because I believe it. I've seen it in action in the lives of plenty of other people. And I'm confident you'll see it in your life before too long." He smiled as he picked up his plate and stood to take it to the kitchen. "End of sermon."

After helping to clear the table, Dad, Pastor Ewen, and Nathan disappeared into the front room to discuss whatever men discuss while women are doing dishes—which is exactly what Ma, Mrs. Ewen, and I busied ourselves doing.

"How are you adjusting to Colorado?" Mrs. Ewen asked Ma. "More to the point, how are you adjusting to being married again?"

I could tell by the way my mother answered Mrs. Ewen that she felt comfortable here. Strangely, so did I. I would have expected a pastor and his wife to be anything but real—not the way these two people were real. I suspected that I would have enjoyed our lunch with them even if Nathan hadn't been there, though I was definitely glad he had been.

"I just want you to know, Stephanie,"—Mrs. Ewen smiled as she rehung the dishtowel after we'd finished putting away the dishes—"that my son has never before commented about the way a girl fixes her hair."

"Really," Ma said, keeping her tone flat enough that I couldn't determine whether this information pleased or worried her. Both, maybe. But what surprised me was that I could hardly determine how Mrs. Ewen's comment affected *me*.

I felt embarrassed, of course, and maybe somewhat skeptical. Flattered? Not exactly. Delighted?

Definitely.

Chapter Ten

Two weeks later on a Monday morning, as I stood in the middle of the gymnasium floor, I tried to maintain a decent sense of humor. But Miss Roberts, our P.E. teacher, was behaving almost as immaturely toward me as the rest of the girls, and we hadn't even started choosing up teams yet.

"You have to participate," she told me in front of everyone, "but are you sure you wouldn't rather take a ball and hit it off the wall over there for the class period?"

If she was trying to be helpful, she couldn't have failed more miserably. Who'd want to play against a wall? "That's okay. I'll play."

She shrugged. "If you say so."

"Thank you," I said.

Miss Roberts selected two captains, who began choosing girls for their teams, and, of course, I was picked last.

I didn't mind volleyball as long as I was playing in one of the two back rows because sometimes there would be time enough to actually focus on the ball before it came toward me. But in a position at the net, everything usually happened so quickly that I'd barely see the ball hit before it was in my face—usually arriving at a painful downward angle—and I'd stand there, unable to raise my hands in time to return it.

More than once during play, this happened, and Miss Roberts displayed about as much tolerance for my dilemma as a two year old responding to the words *nighty-night, angel baby* when she doesn't want to go to bed.

"Miss Teale," she said, "I really think it might help you to practice against the wall for a while."

I caught the ball she tossed to me and went to the wall.

Each time my hands touched the ball and it smashed against the cement wall in front of me, I mouthed, "I hate P.E. *I hate P.E.*" Or, "Volleyball's a stupid game, anyway!" Or, "Why do I need to do this to graduate?"

About halfway through the hour, I grew tired of my anger and of hearing the game going on behind me—without me. I tossed the ball in a corner and sat down on the plastic chair that was holding the door to the locker room open.

Just then, one of the boys' track coaches came into the gym, watched the game in progress for a few minutes, and then asked Miss Roberts, "Why isn't Stephanie playing?"

She blew her whistle to halt play. "She's supposed to be practicing at the wall," she replied.

"I got bored," I told him. I stood, retrieved the ball I had tossed aside, and hit it against the wall a few times. Then I threw it down again. "Does that look like fun to you?"

"She can't play," Miss Roberts blurted. "I mean, she's half-blind! How can they expect her—"

"More than half-blind," I heard one of the girls whisper, and then she laughed.

But clearly, the coach didn't find anything humorous about the situation. To Miss Roberts, he said, "You and I will talk about this later." Turning to me, he pulled a key ring out of his pocket, unclipped one of the keys, and handed it to me. "The weight room's empty, Stephanie," he said. "Why don't you go do some leg exercises."

More grateful than I'd ever imagined I could be about being told to do weight training, I hurried out of the gym and down the hall to the weight room. Maybe I'd go chat with Mr. Parisch, the

Special Needs Counselor, during lunch and inquire about the possibility of eliminating P.E. from my class schedule. No doubt Miss Roberts wouldn't object.

I went to the locker room several minutes before the rest of the class would return so that I could shower and get dressed in peace. Fortunately, Miss Roberts kept them several minutes past the usual cutoff time, and everyone was in a hurry to get ready before the bell rang. Miss Roberts didn't harass me, either, though she did fold her arms across her chest and glare at me.

I pretended to be too blind to notice.

By lunch time, it seemed as if the entire student body had heard about the incident between Miss Roberts and the boys' track coach—and about me "playing" volleyball against a wall. I ignored everyone who asked me who had won, and I even laughed once when someone claimed that I'd had an unfair advantage because I could see!

I found Mr. Parisch in his office, whined to him for nearly ten minutes about the injustice of it all, and thanked him profusely when he assured me that he could indeed arrange for me to have an hour in one of the resource rooms or in the library instead of in P.E.

Oddly, I caught myself thanking God for this as I hurried to the cafeteria and bought lunch. I had attended church with my parents on both Sunday mornings since my first visit there, and had been doing a lot of thinking about the things Pastor Ewen had told me . . . but I was still no closer to believing any of it than I had been. I'd begun to recognize, though, that there was a part of me that yearned to believe it. And why not? The idea of an all-powerful God making a way for me to know Him? The idea that such a God would love me? And accept me? Well, if that were true . . .

"Hey, Stephanie," someone behind me said. "It's too bad you weren't here this winter. We could've really used someone like you on the volleyball team."

SNOW

I recognized the voice—Dana Cullen's—and decided not to acknowledge it. I kept walking toward an empty table near the windows as if I'd never heard her, sat down, and started eating the chef's salad I'd selected.

Dana, along with her usual entourage of six to eight friends, followed me. Even though the thought of eating while they all sat around the table with nothing to do but stare and laugh at me turned my stomach, I stayed in my chair and kept putting food into my mouth.

Our track teams had participated in two city track meets during the past two weeks, and I had yet to finish the mile ahead of Dana Cullen. I'd won two crisp red ribbons in my two races, but they meant nothing to me. I hadn't even put them in my awards box yet.

"I bet you could have helped us out in basketball too."

"Dana," I said, putting my fork down, "I feel really sorry for you."

Dana stared blankly at me, as did all her friends.

"I mean, if you have to work this hard to convince yourself that you're better than *me*, then——"

Dana laughed, just as I knew she would. "Name one thing you're better at than I am," she challenged.

"She's better at *this*," one of her friends said, picking up one of her textbooks, opening it, and holding it right in front of her face to read aloud one slow word at a time.

"And this," another girl said, squinting her eyes until her entire face scrunched up.

"And she wouldn't have to powder her face white to do pantomime!" a third interjected, laughing.

Just as I was about to stand up and leave the table, biting back sarcastic comments about diapers and time-outs for naughty and insensitive children, I felt a hand on my shoulder and heard Nathan Ewen tell Dana, "For one thing, she's a lot nicer than you are."

At first, Dana looked shocked, as if she couldn't believe that Nathan would defend me at her expense. But then her expression changed back to her customary sneer, and she said, "Oh, you're just saying that because it's the good Christian thing to do, Nathan. You saw her. She couldn't think of one thing."

I knew that what I wanted to do next was mean, spiteful, and unfair, and I almost managed to keep my mouth shut again and not do it. But Dana's smugness and her persistent teasing had gotten to me. Slowly, quietly, I said, "Well, there is goalball."

"Goalball?" she asked. "I've never heard of it. What is it?"

"Oh," I said, shrugging, "it's a game blind people play." I purposefully made my voice pathetic and declined to give her any details about the nature of the game or its rules. "I can show you," I suggested. "Tomorrow during lunch? In the gym."

"Anything blind people can do, Dana can do . . . whatever it is."

This was exactly the attitude I'd been hoping for.

I looked from Dana's friend back to Dana, waiting to see if she shared her friend's ignorant and arrogant confidence. Apparently so. Her posture and her expression had not changed except that she'd begun to smile—and not the kind of smile you use when you want someone to know she's special to you.

Perfect.

"Tomorrow in the gym, then." Dana stood up with her friends, and all of them left the table.

"Don't wear shorts!" I called to them.

Nathan sat beside me. "So . . . what is goalball?"

"Are you willing to give up your lunch tomorrow?" I asked him, smiling.

He nodded.

So I told him all about goalball—the rules, the object, the most effective strategies. I drew a diagram of the court for him. "Even though there're supposed to be three players on a team," I said when I'd finished with my explanation of the game, "Dana and I can play one-on-one."

Nathan stared thoughtfully down at the sheet of paper on the table. "I don't know if she'll go for this once she finds out she has to be blindfolded."

"Then she's a coward, and we'll both know it. She's the one who's so proud she can do anything blind people can do."

"Well . . . Stephanie, you have to admit that you'll have a pretty significant advantage."

I squinted at Nathan. "Whose side are you on? Who do you think has the significant advantage when I have to play volleyball?"

"That's true. But—"

I grabbed my sheet of paper and stuffed it into my book bag. Then I stood up. "If you don't want to help me, Nathan, just say so."

"I'll help you." He stood up too, and we walked out of the cafeteria. "It's just . . . you know that when she loses she's just going to shrug it off. It's not as if anyone will be watching. And goalball's just a 'blind people' game that nobody 'normal' cares about."

I stopped walking and glared at him. "Is that what you think?"

"No," he said without hesitation. "That's what she'll think." Then he glared at me. "If you don't know by now that I don't think that way, then—"

"I'm sorry," I said as I started walking again. I did know that he didn't think that way. "I shouldn't have said that."

"That's right. You shouldn't have."

I shouldn't have. In the three weeks since starting at Canyon Street High, I'd learned a lot about Nathan Ewen. He loved his God. He was extremely aggressive about his running. He was an honest friend. He listened exclusively to Christian music. His favorite dinner was pork chops and potatoes au gratin. And . . . it didn't take much to irritate him.

He wasn't extremely skilled at hiding it when someone *had* irritated him, either. And I had.

We'd walked up the stairs to the second floor and all the way to my classroom before he spoke again. "Do you have all the gear you'll need for tomorrow?"

I nodded. "Nathan, I'm—"

"Forget it." He turned quickly and walked away.

Wonderful. Now I'd made the one friend I did have in this school mad at me. I'd done exactly what Ma had warned me about. I'd second-guessed Nathan's friendship—which had, as she'd foreseen, offended him.

It didn't matter how much I tried to convince myself that he was the one in the wrong. That he shouldn't be offended. If only he knew how difficult it was for me to believe that someone like him would accept me! It didn't matter because—and this was the first time that I could remember admitting this without attempting to justify it—I'd been a jerk, and I knew it.

And there was no way I was going to "forget it."

Chapter Eleven

Because the school staff person I'd spoken with had seemed less than eager to have me put tape down on the gymnasium floor, I didn't tape around the whole court. In fact, instead of tape in the one playing area that I did mark out, I used thick string, taped only at the corners. It wasn't as if we were actually going to be playing goalball, anyway.

"This is heavy," Nathan said, tossing my goalball on his palms. The bells inside it jingled a bit. "Doesn't it hurt when it hits you?"

I smiled. "Depends on where it hits you."

He thought about that. "How do you make sure it won't hit you where it'll hurt?"

"Practice," I said. "But even then, it still does sometimes. Such are the hazards of diving to stop a ball you can't see."

"I guess so." He smiled and handed the ball back to me. "So, what do you want me to do?"

"Well, I agree with you that it wouldn't be fair for Dana and me to actually play against one another, so I set up just one play area. She can throw the ball at me first . . . I was thinking of ten throws each? Then I'll take my blindfold off, give it to her, and I'll throw the ball for her to stop."

"You'll be nice, I hope?"

"Yes," I said, somewhat grudgingly. I didn't want to be nice to Dana Cullen, but I didn't want to break her nose, either. "I'll be nice. I'll show her everything before we start. How to throw the ball low to the ground so that it doesn't bounce much—which makes it a whole lot easier for your opponents to hear. I'll show her how to slide in the direction she thinks the ball is coming. I'll show her how to figure out where she is on the court by feeling the string on the floor. And I'll even show her how to cover her face with her arm in case she catches the ball there."

"So when you're really playing this game," Nathan said, "you have three people on each side of the court, in this taped-off playing area. The center person stands in front, the two others on either side behind?"

"Yeah."

"Then, when the other team hurls the ball toward you, you all dive for it, sliding on your sides in the direction you think the ball's coming?"

"Mm-hmm."

"How do you keep from smacking into your teammates?"

I laughed. "Practice, Nathan. Like I told you. It's a lot easier than it sounds once you've done it a few times."

He nodded, but it seemed that he didn't know whether or not to believe me. "Then someone on your team rolls the ball back to the other end of the court, hoping to slide it past the other team's three players."

"Right."

"Do people ever throw it in a totally wrong direction?"

Embarrassing memories besieged my mind. "Yeah. But as you play more, you get better at orienting yourself by using the tape and by listening for movement at the other end of the court." I grinned. "Really, Nathan, it's not as hard as it sounds."

"I can't imagine eating a bowl of cereal without being able to see what I was doing," he said seriously, "let alone functioning as part of a team with this ball flying toward me every few seconds."

"Well," I said, "maybe that's why this God of yours allowed you to be born with good eyesight." I grinned. "Maybe He knew you'd cave under the challenge and wind up sitting in a corner somewhere feeling sorry for yourself."

He grinned right back at me. "You don't know me very well, do you?"

"No," I admitted. "And I'm not an expert on God, either. I was just trying to be funny." Actually, I'd been thinking quite a bit lately about God, and why He'd allow one person the privilege of being born with perfect vision—perfect health in any form—while denying it from so many others. It didn't make much sense to me. Maybe He allowed it for no other reason than to make people think about Him. Maybe it could show the world how strong He is if a person with handicaps could really learn to be happy with who she was. Maybe.

Or maybe He simply had a bad sense of humor.

Or maybe He'd had nothing to do with it. If I didn't want to give Him credit for the good things in my life, I certainly shouldn't be so eager to blame Him for the bad.

Especially if He didn't even exist!

But I had to be honest with myself. I'd been too intrigued and frightened recently by the possibility that He did exist to keep hardening myself against it the way I always had. He did exist. I knew it. Somehow. Somewhere inside. I knew it. Now all I had to do was decide whether or not I could love a God who'd made me—and so many others—differently than He'd made everyone else.

"What I need you to do," I told Nathan, "is round up the ball after it's been thrown—because Dana will probably never stop it."

"What if she does?" he asked quietly, and I knew he wasn't wanting to know what he should do about the ball.

SNOW

"Then I won't have proved my point, or myself, and this whole thing will have been a less than sweet waste of time." I smiled. "But she won't. Not more times than I will, anyway." I was standing close enough to Nathan at that moment to see his expression clearly—and I didn't like it. "Come on, Nathan," I snapped, "you don't seriously think she's going to walk in here and be able to do this just like that!"

"I don't think," he said, "that you should have your self-esteem riding on this, no matter how Dana does."

"Oh you don't." I stepped away from him. "Just what would you have me base my self-esteem on, then? My great looks? How well I fit in with the rest of society? What?"

Nathan didn't have a chance to answer because Mr. Parisch entered the gym, followed by Dana and several of her friends. But Nathan didn't need to speak in order to fully communicate his displeasure at my comments, and apparently he didn't mind expressing it in front of an audience. His entire posture stiffened as he glared at me and breathed out slowly—and loudly— through his nose. Then he walked away from me to stand by himself behind the playing area I'd marked off without greeting anyone, even though he walked right by them.

I didn't have time just then to attempt to appease him.

After explaining all the concepts, objects, rules, strategies, and hints about goalball that I could think of, I said, "I'll go first, and then Dana can give it a shot. Whichever one of us is scored upon the fewest number of times wins." I paused. "Okay?"

Dana only laughed. "You've got to be kidding. You're kidding, right? I mean, this isn't really a game, is it? I mean, you're crazy if you think I'm going to throw myself on the floor to stop a ball I can't see!"

"I wasn't the one who said you could do anything a blind person can," I reminded her.

She took a second or two to consider that before reminding me that she hadn't said it either. And then, after shaking her head and telling me again that I had to be crazy, Dana left the gym. Her friends, of course, left with her. Mr. Parisch stayed around long enough to assure me that he would have enjoyed seeing how the game worked, but then he left too, eager to "grab some lunch" on the way back to his office.

I stood in front of the empty doorway, worried because I knew that even though Dana had turned out to be too much of a coward to even try to beat me, I was the one who would wind up looking like The Supreme Loser in everyone's eyes.

Hadn't Nathan tried to tell me this would happen?

Nathan. I'd almost forgotten that he was still in the gym. Slowly, half-afraid of what he'd say to me, I turned and approached him. When he said nothing, I stared nervously down at the blindfold in my hands. "I guess you're thinking *I told you so*, huh?"

"I'm too angry to tell you what I'm thinking right now," he said, not smiling. Then he picked up the goalball, walked across the gym, and stood there facing me. "Let me see you stop this thing."

Usually, I could discern a person's intent in his tone, but not now. Was Nathan still angry at me? Was he trying to console me? Humor me? Tease me? Beyond the obvious—a goalball demonstration—I had no way of knowing what he was after, or why. But I took my position behind the string on the floor, put on my blindfold, and bent slightly at the knees so that I'd be lower to the floor when he rolled the ball.

He didn't say a word.

Unable to see anything, I stood completely still, waiting. Waiting for that slight and telling sound of the bells shifting inside the ball. It would happen when the person getting ready to throw the ball tightened his hold on it and pulled it backward before letting go right above the floor. Once that sound came, I'd listen for a split second for the whispered hum of the rubber ball as it moved across the wood floor, trying to determine its angle, its speed, and where it would cross the line on my side of the court—all in that one instant before I'd have to commit my body to slide either left or right.

Though I'd learned to be effective on a goalball court, I'd never quite grown comfortable with the complete blackness behind my blindfold. I might not be able to see much compared to the average person, but I *could* see, and to suddenly be so limited was unnerving. Especially since a ball roughly the size of a soccer ball—but firmer and heavier—was about to be bowled toward me.

"Throw it, already," I said.

He did. So slowly that I probably could have stopped it without stretching out on my side and sliding. But I did slide left, head first, taking care to keep my arms—which were stretched straight above my head—taut and shoulder width apart so that they'd block the ball and not just provide a speed bump on the way to the goal line. I kept my legs straight and shoulder width apart too, for the same reason. The ball hit my thighs—one of the better places on the body for stopping a goalball if avoiding pain was a consideration.

Quickly I grabbed the ball, got to my feet, and tossed it back toward Nathan. When I heard him pick it up and stop walking when he got to the spot he planned to throw from, I said, "The sixth grade girls at the blind school throw harder than you just did, Nathan." I didn't want him to be afraid of hurting me. And I suspected he'd never throw hard enough without a little provocation. "Don't be thinking you have to be gentle because I'm a poor little blind girl."

That worked . . . he threw the ball hard and fast . . . I almost failed to get to it on time. But that time, and each of the other eight times he threw it, I did stop it. After the tenth shot, I pulled off the blindfold, picked up the ball, and walked across the gym toward him.

He met me in the middle. "Ten for ten," he said. "Not bad." He took the blindfold from my hands. "My turn."

"You don't have to—"

He stared at me, still without a smile. "I want to."

I shrugged. "Suit yourself." After helping him figure out how to stay oriented on the court once he'd put the blindfold on, I hurried across the gym and threw the ball.

He missed it, of course. But he had moved in the right direction, so I encouraged him to try again . . . which he did. Four times with the same result. But then on my sixth toss, he put himself exactly where he needed to be to stop the ball. His body wasn't exactly parallel to the string on the floor—which is a plus in actual play unless you don't mind the pain and momentary embarrassment of colliding with your team members. Nor was he perfectly perpendicular to the floor itself. But he had stopped the ball—and in goalball, that's what matters most.

"Good job, Nathan!"

After moving his hand along the string in front of him until he found the *T* that marked the center of the playing area, he stood and tossed the ball back to me. "Four more," he said, more to himself than to me.

He stopped the next two throws easily.

As soon as I let go of the ball on my ninth throw and saw him lie down without sliding because I'd thrown it right up the center of the court, I shouted, "Tighten your stomach, Nathan, or it's going to—" But I couldn't speak quickly enough. I heard the ball smack into him, and then I heard him gasp in for air and get none. "—hurt," I finished uselessly, cringing at the memory of my first—and last—save on a soft stomach. "Sorry."

He stood slowly and rolled the ball back to me. "One more."

I expected, when I threw the ball, to see him react to it with less boldness than he had been. Instead, he seemed even more determined to stop it. He threw himself toward the sound of the bells and the ball coming toward him—-and he did stop it—-with his face.

I had never done that personally, but I'd seen it happen to others more than once. As Nathan pushed the ball away from himself and rolled onto his back to cover his face with his hands, I ran across the gym and sat down beside him.

"Are you all right?" Gently, I pulled his hands back, lifted the blindfold away, and, relieved, smiled. "No blood," I said. "This girl on Denmark's team got hit in the face during a game I was watching when we were competing in Europe, and—"

Nathan pulled away from me and got quickly to his feet. "There," he nearly shouted. "You got to prove yourself after all. You stopped ten. I stopped five. You're better than me. Are you happy?" And then, without giving me an opportunity to respond, he left.

I peeled up tape and gathered the string, the goalball, the blindfold, and the other equipment I'd brought and shoved it back into my treasured *Team USA* bag. No, Nathan, I thought, I'm not happy.

Chapter Twelve

As I walked toward home after track training that afternoon, I couldn't help feeling angry. Angry at Dana. Angry at Nathan. But mostly, angry at myself. Had I really expected to find some satisfaction, some self-worth, in performing better at goalball than a fully sighted person who'd never heard of the game or seen it played? Even if I didn't fully understand the motivation behind Nathan's outburst—*You're better than me. Are you happy?*— I couldn't dismiss the nagging certainty that I'd earned it.

A car slowed to a stop beside me. A pickup, actually. Red.

"Stephanie, it's Nathan." The passenger door opened next to me. "Want a ride home?"

Unable to keep from smiling, I climbed into the passenger seat and pulled the door shut. As Nathan pulled the truck into the street again, I said, "Thanks for identifying yourself. Would have saved me a heart attack if I hadn't already recognized your truck."

He nodded. "I didn't know if you'd paid attention to the truck the last time I drove you home. Girls don't always pay attention."

I wanted to thank him for that. For realizing that there might be reasons for a visually impaired person failing to notice things—other than having poor eyesight. But I said nothing. It would probably come out sounding stupid, anyway. I'd been stupid enough already for one day.

Besides, I *had* noticed his truck.

"Listen Stephanie," he said right away, "I'm sorry about the way I acted today. It just . . . seeing the way you cut yourself down all the time . . . it just got to me, I guess." He shrugged. "You've probably figured out by now that I don't have the most level temperament in the world . . . and catching that last ball with my face didn't help much when I was already angry."

"It's all right," I said, "now that I know why you were upset. But, Nathan, you've seen how people treat me. After so many years of hearing that all the time, a person just . . . starts to believe it."

"Well, you should figure out a way *not* to believe it because you're a great person. You're fun to be around—when you're not cutting yourself down."

Since I didn't know how to handle his compliment, I said, "And you should figure out a way to soften your temper a little. You're a lot more fun to be around when you're not pouting."

"I don't pout."

I laughed.

"I don't pout."

"Whatever, Nathan."

"I don't pout." He stayed quiet awhile. "Okay. I don't hide it when I'm mad." He looked at me as he pulled the truck to a stop at a red light. "We don't have a track meet the weekend of spring break, so Judah and Rebekah and I are going up to the mountains for some four-wheel driving. My sister will be home then, but she already said she doesn't want to go—she hates four-wheel driving—so we have an empty seat. Would you be interested in coming with us?"

I nodded. "Sure. Sounds like fun. If you're sure Judah and Rebekah won't mind me—"

"There you go again. Cutting yourself down. Why would they mind?"

The truth was, when I stopped and thought about it, I couldn't think of a reason for them to mind my coming along. Not one. So I said, "Okay, then. I'd love to go."

Nathan smiled. "That's what I wanted to hear in the first place."

When we arrived at my house a few minutes later and I climbed out of the truck, I said, "Thanks for the invitation, Nathan."

He grinned. "Don't thank me until we're home safe. I hope the roads don't scare you."

I shrugged. "My father and I have been up there a few times."

"Good," he said. "See you tomorrow?"

"Yeah."

All that afternoon, and for the next week and a half, I couldn't seem to think about anything but Nathan's invitation. I had never before been invited anywhere by a boy. Even though I knew that there was nothing romantic about the invitation, and that I probably would be frightened by many of the rough high-mountain roads we'd undoubtedly be traveling, I had no doubt that the day was going to be one I'd never forget.

"What do you think I should wear?" I asked Ma two nights before the trip.

Sighing, she sat beside me on my bed. "What, Stephanie? None of the suggestions I made the other three-hundred-and-six times have suited you?"

"I haven't asked you that many times," I said, even though I knew I had. "I'm sorry, Ma."

"It's all right." She stood and opened my closet door. "Wear something comfortable. Wear a hat. Wear shoes you can walk around on rocks in. Don't forget your sunscreen."

"No, Ma. That's not what I was asking. What color should I wear? Which top? Which—?"

SNOW

"Stephanie, you're going four-wheel driving. Wear jeans and a sweatshirt!"

I laughed. "Okay. Okay. Sorry."

Ma hugged me and started to leave the room.

"What should I do with my hair?"

Ma stared at the ceiling for a moment, moaning like the furnace fan when it needed to be replaced.

"You shouldn't complain," I told her. "If I was normal, you'd be going through this every single weekend."

Turning to face me, no longer moaning, Ma reached out and gently touched my hair. "Put it in a French braid. Nathan seemed to like it that way . . . remember?"

I nodded. I remembered.

So she does understand.

It took a deliberate effort on my part, but I didn't mention the four-wheel driving trip during dinner that night, or during my chess game with Dad afterward. And I had every intention of not talking about it with Katie again during Choir the next morning—she was probably sick of hearing about it too . . . But the first thing she said to me when I walked through the door was "So, are you excited about tomorrow?"

And far be it from me to be rude and not reply!

Chapter Thirteen

For the first time in a long time, I was actually hungry for lunch that Friday. I hurried to the cafeteria, excited about the trip the next day, but also looking forward to seeing Nathan. Listening to my mother's advice had certainly paid off when it came to Nathan. I'd finally made a "normal" friend whose motives I no longer felt the need to question.

The cafeteria was unusually crowded—probably because of the rainy weather. I bought a taco salad and began weaving my way through the tables in search of a place to sit. After attempting to take a chair at three different tables and being told, "That seat's saved," all three times, I heard someone say, "Hey, Ewen," a couple of tables over and started walking that way. If there was an empty seat beside Nathan, *he* wouldn't tell me it was saved.

As I got closer, I realized that Nathan already had company for lunch. I could hear their voices—Dana Cullen, Brit, and a couple of boys from the track team. I could hear their conversation.

"Is it a date, Nathan?"

"No."

Dana giggled. "Katie said that you two are going with your brother and his girlfriend. Sounds like a date to me."

"It's not a date," Nathan insisted. "I'm not even allowed to date yet!"

SNOW

"Ewen and the Snow Princess," one of the guys said, laughing. "Who'd have thought?"

"Shut up," Nathan snapped.

He sounded angry.

And embarrassed.

Dana giggled again. "What do you see in her, Nathan? I mean, do you want your kids to turn out like——"

"Shut up!" he said again. "I invited her because I feel sorry for her. You know? Because she doesn't have any friends here and you guys are all such jerks to her. Anyway, she's—"

But he stopped talking then because he saw me.

"Hi, Stephanie," Dana said. "You can have my seat if you want. I've got to go."

"See you later, Ewen," one of the guys said as he too stood and left. The other boy followed him. Neither of them had the decency to wait until they'd gotten to the end of the table to start laughing.

As quietly as I could under the circumstances, I set my tray on the table. I did not, however, sit down.

"You heard us," Nathan said.

Ignoring the urge to spout off every remark I'd ever heard a blind person make about having excellent hearing to compensate for the lack of vision, I said nothing.

"Stephanie—"

I held up my hands. "Don't bother, Nathan. And don't come to pick me up tomorrow. I've decided to stay home." And then, before I either said something I'd later regret or started to cry like an idiot, I ran out of the cafeteria and didn't stop running until I slammed through the door of the nearest girls' restroom. How had this happened—and why was it bothering me so much? Why had Katie talked to Dana Cullen about my plans for tomorrow? What gave Dana and the others any right to harass Nathan about them? Why hadn't he defended me?

Because he was embarrassed. The idea that other kids thought he might like me had embarrassed him.

And not only that.

He'd admitted it himself . . . his kindness to me, his invitation for tomorrow, his friendship, had all been extended to me because of pity. Nothing more.

So much for Ma's advice.

After washing my face until I felt in control again, drying it with a handful of paper towels, and brushing my hair, I left the bathroom. I didn't want Nathan's pity. I didn't need it. I didn't need *him*. If all he had to offer was a friendship based on pity, then I could live without it, thank you very much.

Nice pep talk, I congratulated myself. Too bad I didn't really believe it. Life would be a lot easier if I did.

"Stephanie?"

I recognized Nathan's voice behind me and kept walking straight ahead.

He grabbed my arm. "Come on, Stephanie. Just hear me out."

"You'd better make it fast," I said as I spitefully turned to face him. "The five-minute bell's about to ring."

"I'm sorry," he said. Then he stood there, waiting for me to say something.

I did. "That was fast, all right."

When he said nothing more, I turned to walk away again.

"Wait."

I stopped walking but did not look at him.

"I know what you're thinking," he said. "How it looks. But it didn't come out how I meant it . . . exactly."

Now I faced him. "And how, exactly, did you mean it? It sounded plain enough to me."

"I do feel sorry for you," he said. "Is that a crime? People are mean to you so, yeah, I feel sorry for you. And I'm not going to apologize for that."

"Yeah, well, save your pity for someone—"

"What I am apologizing for is letting them embarrass me into trying to explain away our friendship as something less than it is so they wouldn't think it was something more than it is." He looked toward the ceiling and shook his head. "That isn't what I meant either . . . exactly."

Even though I didn't want to do it, I smiled. "When you figure it out, let me know, okay?" Seriously, I added, "I think I understand."

We started walking together toward the stairs.

"It isn't that I couldn't like you the way they were saying I like you," he said quickly and nervously, "but since, you know . . . You know what? I'm just going to shut up now, okay? How does that sound?"

I laughed and shrugged. He could have kept talking. It wouldn't have bothered me. But he didn't say anything more about what had happened in the lunchroom, and I didn't press him. He had apologized. He had made his reasoning clear . . . well, not exactly . . . but clear enough for me to know that his feeling sorry for me was a result of our friendship and not the root of it.

That was good enough for me. "Nathan? I would still like to go tomorrow if—"

"You bet," he said. "I was just going to ask you about that."

My three remaining classes that afternoon passed as a painfully slow blur in which my mind was even less focused than my eyes . . . when it came to schoolwork, anyway.

Chapter Fourteen

The day was crisp and cloudless. After stopping at the drive-thru at a fast-food place to pick up breakfast on our way out of town, Judah, Rebekah, Nathan, and I headed west toward the mountains. Good-mornings had been exchanged, a general plan for the day had been agreed upon, and there was nothing left to do but sit back, enjoy the scenery, and listen to Nathan and his brother talk about cars . . . which they did for nearly an hour.

But I didn't mind.

Rebekah, however, did. "Are you ready for all your finals?" she asked Judah, interrupting him in the middle of his second *You'll have to make sure you get a four-wheel drive when you buy your own car, Nathan* mini-sermon.

He laughed. "Sorry. I think so."

And then Judah and Rebekah talked about their final term papers for Senior English until we turned off the highway onto a gravel road that would eventually deteriorate into a rough four-wheel-drive road.

" 'Warning,' " Nathan read aloud as we passed by a sign, " 'this road is not maintained beyond Thunder Lake. Use caution.' "

"The things I do for you," Rebekah said jokingly to Judah.

"Anyone need to stop at the rest area?" Judah asked, slowing the Jeep beside a couple of rundown-looking outhouses in the trees. "This is the last civilization for a while."

I laughed. "This is civilization?"

Not surprisingly, nobody cared to take advantage of the rest stop.

We drove by a small lake, and Judah shifted into low gear at the start of what he called the "real road." But I wouldn't call it that. Two dirt tracks in the rock-speckled grass. Within only a few minutes, boulders, felled trees, ruts, mud holes, steep hills, and tight corners made the ride slow, bumpy, and nauseating. "Have you been up here before, Stephanie?" he asked me.

"No," I told him. "Not on this road."

"It goes to an old mining town," he said. "Old cabins and a mine shaft, almost at the top of the mountain. The view is . . . "

"Gorgeous," Nathan finished for his brother, who had probably let his sentence trail off because he realized he was talking to someone who may or may not care about the view and then felt uncomfortable about having brought it up.

Fortunately, mountains were big enough that I could enjoy the view—at least to a certain degree.

"There's still plenty of snow up here," Rebekah said. "I doubt we'll be able to get all the way up the road this early in the year."

Judah nodded. "We'll just go as far as we can and then turn around."

"I want to drive," Nathan said, leaning forward to nudge his brother.

Judah only laughed. "If you knew how much of my paycheck goes to making the payments and insurance on this thing, you wouldn't even ask."

"Yeah, but I don't know," Nathan pointed out. "So can I drive?"

"I'll think about it," was all Judah would promise. "You could get a job, you know, and then you could buy your own four-wheel—"

"I'm starved," Rebekah announced, giggling as she interrupted Judah again. "Let's stop to eat."

"Very funny." Judah turned to grin at Rebekah, but quickly turned his attention back to the road when his front axle scraped against a boulder.

"Come on, Judah," Nathan pressed. "Let me drive."

Judah backed the Jeep up to try to negotiate his way up and over the rock from a different angle. He didn't acknowledge his brother.

Leaning across me to study the road through my passenger side window, Nathan said, "Drive your right front tire right over the middle of it and then turn the wheel sharp to the left."

Judah did as his brother suggested. The transmission whined, the tire slipped a bit, and the entire vehicle went way crosswise, but we made it over the rock without banging the axle again. Before Judah had even loosened his grip on the steering wheel, Nathan was at him again to let him drive.

I said, "Hey, Judah, at least you know that *I* won't be bugging you about driving."

Nathan sat back in his seat, suddenly so captivated by something outside his window that he wouldn't look anywhere else.

"You're pouting," I whispered to him.

He ignored me.

"You haven't driven this kind of road before, Stephanie?" Judah asked me.

"I haven't driven before, period."

"That's right," he muttered. "Sorry."

"It's okay," I assured him. "My father and I come up here sometimes, and he mumbles to himself about how to get over this rock without getting hung up on that one or going so far to the right of the road that that branch over there won't scratch up the paint job. I think I understand the strategy, but there's no way I'd be able to pick my way through this stuff."

Judah drove over another intimidating patch of boulders on the way down to cross a stream of melt-off that had washed away the road and then over an even more challenging collection of them to get back up. Then he said, "What if something happened to your dad while you two were up here?"

It wasn't as though the thought had never occurred to me. "I'd stand on the biggest boulder I could find and scream like an idiot until someone heard me," I answered, only half-joking.

Nobody spoke for several minutes. Judah's Jeep crawled steadily up the road until he had to pull it into a narrow patch of snow-covered grass to clear the trail for "traffic" coming down. Three four-wheelers and a dog. We'd seen their pickup trucks and trailers at the bottom of the road.

Judah opened his window and asked the driver of the first four-wheeler how the road looked up ahead. The smell of pine pushed its way inside on icy air. After a few minutes of conversation about snow banks, slick corners, and *you must have gotten up early to be heading down already*, we were back on the road—each of us having put on the coat we'd brought along.

"It's cold up here," Rebekah commented.

Judah nodded and turned up the heat. "That's one thing about Colorado, Stephanie," he said. "You can't go too far without running into someone . . . even up here. Still, you should know how to drive just in case you ever had to."

"It's illegal. And even if it wasn't . . . " I laughed. "I'd kill us for sure."

"Nah." Judah shook his head. "If your dad has a four-wheel drive like mine, you can put it in the lowest gear, and it won't let the vehicle move faster than five or six miles per hour. You could just creep down the trail. You can see the road, right?"

"Yeah."

"Even if you banged up the underside a little . . . "

"Well," I said, anxious to stop thinking about the kinds of circumstances that would require me to drive my father down a mountain, "my mother is here now. She'd be with us. And the chances of something happening to both of them—"

"You should know how to drive just in case."

I laughed. "Judah, you're morbid. Anyway, who's going to risk his vehicle on a road like this to teach me?"

After only the slightest hesitation, Judah said, "I will."

"Oh, that's just great," Nathan complained beside me. "You won't let me drive, but you'll let someone who can barely see the road?"

Both Rebekah and Judah stiffened at Nathan's seeming insensitivity, but I laughed aloud. If Nathan felt comfortable enough with the reality of my low vision to make a comment like that without apology, then I must have gained some ground in earning true acceptance from him. It was a fact that I could barely see the road. Why apologize about saying so? "It *is* kind of inconsistent on your part," I said to Judah.

"Thank you," Nathan said, smiling apprehensively.

Judah stopped the Jeep and opened his door. "Beck, would you get in back with Nathan?" He patted the steering wheel. "Come up here, Stephanie."

"No." I shook my head. "Thanks, but . . . no."

"I'll be sitting right next to you," Judah said, prodding me. "I'll grab the wheel if it looks like you're about to get in trouble." He gave me a moment to consider. "Come on."

"Listen, I appreciate what you're trying to do . . . " And I did. "But . . . what if I hurt the Jeep somehow? We'll be stuck. If we had another vehicle along, then, yeah, I might—"

"Now there's an excuse I wouldn't have thought of," Nathan said, patting my shoulder.

"It's not an excuse." I felt my face flush as I grinned. "It's a reason."

"Mm-hmm."

Rebekah opened her door, climbed out of the Jeep, and leaned her seat forward. "I think you're outnumbered," she said to me.

"Come on, guys," I said, seriously frightened by the prospect of getting behind the wheel of someone else's vehicle on a road like the one that we were on. "I don't want to do this."

Judah stared thoughtfully at me for a second before getting back into his seat. "Okay," he said easily. "The guy on the four-wheeler said we'd only be able to get another two miles or so up the road before we won't be able to get through the snowdrifts. What do you say we get up as far as we can, eat lunch, head down, and see if we have time to try another road?"

"Sounds good to me," Rebekah said, pulling her door shut again and buckling her seat belt.

"Me too." Nathan leaned over the back of his seat to dig around in the cooler. "What'd you bring for lunch, anyway?"

And that was that. End of conversation. No pressure. No disappointment. Nobody would mention it again. They wouldn't make me try to drive if I didn't want to.

But the real problem was not that I didn't want to drive . . . it was that I didn't think I'd be able to do it. I was afraid. Rightfully so? Maybe. Maybe not. I couldn't stop thinking that Dad and I would be up here alone again. Ma was not the type to enjoy four-wheel driving, and Dad was not the type to be content with putting around in figure eights through National Forest campgrounds.

It took us almost an hour to reach the spot where the road disappeared beneath a huge snow bank. A set of tire tracks marred it for about two hundred feet, but beyond that, it remained untreaded and impassable.

Nathan climbed out of the Jeep behind Judah and shut the door. "I wonder how long it took that guy to dig himself out of there."

Pointing to the mounds of snow all around the spot where the tire tracks abruptly ended, Judah said, "Looks like he was stuck pretty good."

"Hope he had a shovel." Rebekah shook her head. "Some people think they can do anything."

And then there's me, I thought. Most of the time, being legally blind didn't bother me too much—not as much as looking different bothered me. But sometimes—times like now—I hated having low vision. If I could see well, I wouldn't give a second thought to driving Judah's Jeep down this mountain. In fact, if I could see well, I'd probably have my own four-wheel drive, and Nathan would be riding with me!

Rebekah opened the cooler and set out the crackers, cheeses, sliced summer sausage, and veggie sticks she had prepared. We prayed, and then we ate—standing near the Jeep because the ground was too wet to sit on. The air off the snow all around us turned our faces red and numbed our fingers, but it was just too beautiful a day to spend it all inside the car. The sun was shining so brightly that all the colors looked extra crisp. The blue of the sky. The green of the pine trees visible all the way down the mountainside and on the slope directly across the valley. The white glare of the snow—blinding, almost. Even the colors of our clothes seemed more vibrant up here.

But it was cold, so we ignored the temptation to have a snowball fight and hurried to climb back into the warm Jeep.

Because of the steep hills on both sides of the road, getting turned around again was a challenge. But Judah managed it. Then he surrendered the driver's seat to Nathan, saying, "I worked closing last night." He buckled in next to me, leaned his head against the window, and was asleep within minutes.

"See, he trusts you," Rebekah said to Nathan.

"Nah. He just doesn't want to be awake to watch me."

I did notice, as we made our way down the mountain, that Nathan wasn't as conservative a driver as his older brother. He drove faster. He took less care about the boulders in the road. He hit mud holes on purpose. And once or twice, he went out of his way for the challenge of a rut or a boulder configuration he just couldn't resist—all within the boundaries of the trail, of course. I was glad to see that the Ewens respected the same *No off-roading off the off-road* philosophy that my father had taught me.

I decided after about half an hour of straining to keep my head straight because the ride was so bumpy that I preferred Judah's approach to mastering these roads. Clearly, Rebekah did too. She asked Nathan several times to slow down. He always did, but never quite enough.

Just when I began to marvel that Judah hadn't been awakened yet by his head banging repeatedly against the window, he muttered, "Hey, Beck, do you want to drive for a while?"

Now Nathan slowed down. Noticeably. Adequately.

I leaned my head from side to side, trying to unknot my muscles.

"Sorry," Nathan said to nobody in particular. He stopped the Jeep to trade seats with Rebekah, and we were off again.

Leaning forward, I watched the road carefully through the front windshield to determine whether or not I could actually see it well enough to drive it. Being limited by my poor vision was one thing. Being limited by fear and insecurity was something else. I *could* distinguish the road from the rest of the ground. I could see the boulders. The dips and angles in the road might be a challenge . . . but Judah had said he'd be right there beside me. I wouldn't have to travel very fast, and I certainly didn't need to worry about oncoming traffic. It wouldn't actually be technically illegal for me to drive here because this wasn't even a registered county road.

The question was whether it would be safe.

I decided it would be . . . and if I got behind the wheel and then realized I'd taken on too much, I could stop. No big deal.

I took in a deep breath. "Judah?"

"Yeah?"

"Would you still show me how to drive . . . if I changed my mind?"

He shrugged. "Sure. Have you changed your mind?"

Slowly I nodded, hoping I looked more resolved than I felt.

"Don't be nervous," Judah said to me when, a few minutes later, I'd buckled in behind the wheel and he'd taken Nathan's spot in the front passenger seat. After familiarizing me with the gas pedal, the brake pedal, the clutch (which he said I'd hardly need to use since we were in low gear), and with the amount of play I'd need to give the wheel to steer the Jeep, he asked, "Ready?"

I looked at my hands on the steering wheel. "How much will I owe you if I wreck this thing?"

"Don't worry," he said evenly, "I won't let that happen."

That was exactly what I wanted to hear.

I did everything Judah told me to do, from stepping on the gas to keeping my front left tire to the right of that rut, from letting off the gas just as we got the rear tires over the top of a dead tree across the road to turning sharply to the left to avoid a pointy boulder. I even got us safely across the stream of snowmelt that had washed out the road. Judah never even reached for the steering wheel. But I was concentrating so much on every movement, every instruction given to me, every noise underneath the Jeep, that I didn't fully enjoy the satisfaction of having done it until we stopped at Thunder Lake where the road returned to gravel and where it would have been illegal for me to drive any farther.

"You did great!" Judah told me. We all walked toward the lake so he could take pictures of the reflection of the snow-covered mountains on the water. "You should be proud of yourself. The first time I did this, I tore the muffler off on a rock."

"And I got us stuck in a major mud hole," Nathan said. "Whew, that was messy . . . but it was fun."

Rebekah smiled. "I'm like you, Stephanie. I don't plan to do this except when I have to." She elbowed Nathan. "Like today—to keep us all from neck injuries!"

"Ha ha ha," Nathan said. "Funny."

The rest of us laughed genuinely . . . at him . . . and it didn't take long for him to join us.

The sense of accomplishment I felt at that moment was equaled only by the sense that I was truly accepted by Nathan, Rebekah, and Judah. Since neither feeling could be adequately put into words, I simply said, "Thanks, guys," hoping they'd understand how much more I meant.

Chapter Fifteen

I could hardly wait to get to church the next morning. Everything seemed to take longer than usual. Boiling water for tea. Getting my hair to cooperate. Choosing my clothes. Breakfast. Even the drive. But finally, after hurrying up the stairs to pull open the glass door for my parents, I was there.

Who'd have thought I'd ever be this excited about going to church?

I asked myself that as we walked up the aisle toward the row we'd made a habit of sitting in. I knew that I wasn't excited about it for the right reasons . . . the reasons that my father would like . . . at least not all of them . . . but I always paid attention to the things Pastor Ewen said, and I never left the building without a healthy dose of Bible-stuff to think about during the week. Sometimes I enjoyed thinking about God—when I could do it on my own terms. More frequently, though, it wasn't happening on my terms. Scriptures Pastor Ewen had quoted or challenges he'd posed wouldn't leave me alone at night . . . and even if I didn't necessarily enjoy this, I'd given up trying to deny my growing curiosity about the truth and my desire to know it.

Still, my main motivation for continuing to attend church with my parents had less to do with God than with the people there. Nathan. Rebekah. Pastor and Mrs. Ewen. Even some of the youth group kids.

For the most part, I felt accepted at church . . . and since I couldn't say the same about school or even the track team,

SNOW

Sunday became my favorite day of the week. Especially since our track meets were usually held on Saturdays and I still hadn't been able to beat Dana Cullen in the mile.

April passed quickly, with only one exception to the normal routine of this new life of mine. Ma had responded to an invitation by Pastor Ewen after his Easter Sunday sermon to accept Christ. She'd become a Christian. And not the *I'm an American, aren't I?* kind of "Christian" either. Like Dad, she was changing. It was real to her . . . in her. I supposed I had expected her to embrace Dad's ideas sooner or later—who could argue with the impact Christianity had had on his life?—but this soon? And so decidedly!

I began to feel a little uncomfortable as the one member of our family still holding out for . . . well, I didn't really know what I was holding out for . . . a miraculous sign? No. A visitation from angels? No. A sudden and inexplicable certainty that God really was and that Christ was the only way to Him? Not exactly. I just wanted to know that this Christianity thing was real.

My parents respected that—though our dinner table conversations increasingly centered on and reflected their faith. I didn't mind. Especially considering what our dinner table conversations might have been had Ma and Dad started to fight again.

On the first Sunday in May, though, neither God nor Ma's new commitment was on my mind as I walked into the sanctuary and sat down beside Nathan. The senior class at Canyon Street High had elected—as a sign that they were modern Americans in favor of Women's Equality Rights—to designate this year's Junior-Senior Prom as a Girl asks Guy (and then pays for everything) event. Not exactly my idea of what's most romantic, but it guaranteed that I'd at least have the chance to think about attending a prom . . . something I'd given up all hope of doing, years ago.

I'd already decided who I wanted to ask. All that was left now was to put together the nerve to do it.

"I'm sorry you finished second in the mile again yesterday," Nathan said to me after glancing up from his bulletin and saying hello.

I shrugged. I was getting used to it. "Congratulations on your win."

He smiled. Winning was nothing new for him.

"Nathan . . . " I straightened my shoulders and locked my resolve. Even though the dance was still two weeks away, I wanted to know now whether or not he'd go with me so that the wondering and thinking of the right way to ask wouldn't drive me crazy. "Would you go to the prom with me?" When he didn't answer right away, I hurried to add, "I wouldn't normally ask a guy, but, you know, it's—"

"I know," he said.

I looked at his hand on his bulletin, waiting for his answer.

"I'm going to say no," he said finally, quietly. "I . . . I don't go to dances. With anyone."

This surprised me. "You don't?"

He shook his head.

"Why not?"

He shrugged. "I don't think they're fun . . . or smart."

Not smart? I didn't understand.

He paused before answering. "Getting so close to someone you might like isn't exactly God's idea of the way to pursue a relationship," he said at last. "It . . . it kind of puts the emphasis on the wrong things at the wrong time."

That made sense, I supposed.

But could I be certain that this wasn't just a convenient excuse for him to not be seen on a "date" with me?

Yes. I could be certain. Nathan had proved that he didn't mind being seen with me. He had proved his friendship. And I knew him. If he didn't want to go with me because it was *me,* he'd have the guts to admit it.

"Do you understand?" he asked, clearly uncomfortable.

I nodded. "I guess you think I'm stupid for asking."

"No." He shook his head. "That's the thing, Stephanie. I like you. I do. But we . . . well, we don't . . . I guess I just don't want to stir up the wrong feelings between us." He moved forward in his chair a little. "My dad says that people shouldn't date like they do now, just for something to do. Dating's for more than that. It's for finding out if I could marry someone." He looked at me. "Someone who wants the same things I want. Someone who loves God the way I do."

"And I don't," I said, not coldly. It was a fact.

He nodded. "You don't. But even if you did. . ." He took a deep breath. "Friendship is a much better foundation for the start of that kind of relationship than some sensual feeling stirred up by a song or two at a dance."

"Yeah."

It was several moments before he said, "I'm sorry."

"Don't be. I mean, friends are honest with each other, right?"

"Right."

I was disappointed of course, but the fact that Nathan had explained his reasoning to me—especially since I could actually understand it—significantly lessened the sense of rejection I would have expected to be feeling after a *no* from him. I wasn't even angry or resentful about his unwillingness to consider a more-than-friendship relationship with me because I wasn't a Christian. In a strange way, I respected him for it . . . though I didn't necessarily plan to admit that to him. "So what's your secret," I asked him, "in the mile? How do you win all the time?"

He visibly relaxed at the change of subject. "I don't win all the time."

"Almost."

"Almost." He thought about it. "I just hate losing more than I hate the discomfort of pushing myself to the limit to win."

"I hate losing," I said. "Especially to Dana Cullen. But so far, that hasn't helped me beat her."

"Maybe you think about it too much," he offered. "I mean, maybe you've made it so important to beat her that it hinders you from relaxing enough to run your best race."

"Maybe." I nodded. "I do want to beat her . . . and not just for the blue ribbon."

"At the next meet, Stephanie, just forget she's in the race with you."

Not likely, I thought, but I told him I'd try.

Pastor Ewen went to the pulpit then, and I said good-bye to Nathan and hurried to my seat beside my father. The sermon was typically well presented and challenging, but for the first time on a Sunday morning, I caught my mind wandering.

Would Nathan be interested in me as more than a friend if I were a Christian?

Is that what he'd meant?

I supposed I could—

No! Nathan would see right through me if I suddenly decided I needed to serve God too. And even if he didn't, I would know the truth. And so would God. Besides, if "sensual feelings stirred up by a song or two at a dance" were a poor excuse for the foundation of a relationship, how much more an outright lie?

I would not let myself be that pathetic.

If and when I decided to become a Christian, I would permit myself to think again about the possibilities for Nathan and me. In the meantime, I had a perfectly good sermon to listen to.

And a perfectly good friendship to value.

Chapter Sixteen

By Friday morning the week of the prom, conversations at school revolved totally and unalterably around who was taking whom. Girls talking among themselves about who they'd asked. Boys talking among themselves about who'd asked them. Since I was watching it all from the outside, as I'd always suspected I would be, it both annoyed and sickened me. The whole thing seemed like nothing more than a huge and pathetic competition. Of course, everyone tried to hide it beneath smiles and "Oh I'm so glad you're going with Bryan!", but it remained as sharply evident as the smell of chicken bones buried at the bottom of the garbage pail a couple of days after the meal.

But since I knew that I wouldn't be keeping it a secret either, if Nathan Ewen had agreed to go with me, I refrained from groaning aloud at all the whispered and giggled comments.

The last thing I was in the mood for when I sat down next to Katie in Choir was her I'm-leaning-toward-you-like-I'm-your-best-friend question about my plans for the dance.

"I'm not going," I told her flatly, hoping she'd get the hint and drop the subject.

She may have gotten the hint, but she didn't drop the subject. "Are you going to ask anyone?"

I stared at her. As if she'd be the one I'd confide in after she'd told the entire student body about my four-wheel driving trip with

Nathan and his brother! "No." It wasn't a lie. I wasn't *going to* ask anyone. She didn't need to know that I already had.

"I'm sure Nathan would go with you," she said.

I wondered if I mightn't be able to redirect Katie's attention. I decided to use a question of my own. "Who are you going to ask?"

That worked. Katie suddenly lost her desire for chit-chatting, and I took the opportunity to pretend to read my notes from government class before she could change her mind.

The choir director entered the room then with his usual demand for our immediate quiet. " 'Tis the season for concerts," he announced. "All of you will, of course, be participating in our final concert next Thursday. I've decided to ask a little more out of you this year."

Anyone who hadn't already stopped talking did so then. Homework . . . in choir?

"I want each of you, with your music partner, to attend one other music event and put together a review of your experience. We'll share those reviews in class during the last three days of school."

Dana stiffened beside me. "Do we have to go with our music partner?" she asked.

I held my breath and waited for his "No."

But a *yes*—one insistent enough to squelch any more questions or pleas for mercy—came instead.

"You will be graded," the director added. "And it will be at least a grade point deduction if you elect not to do this." He laughed. "It's not as if I've buried you in homework in here!"

Rehearsal passed the same way an hour does when you're waiting to go in and see the dentist. Finally it was over, and as we stood to leave the choir hall, Dana put herself in front of me. "My father would kill me if I didn't get an A in choir," she said.

I nodded. My father wouldn't be too impressed either.

"My sister has a piano recital tonight at the mall," Dana said. "What if I pick you up and we go to that? We might as well get it out of the way."

Again, I nodded.

"Wear something decent," she said, and walked by me.

The only consolation was that being seen with me was probably going to be a whole lot harder on Dana than putting up with her was going to be on me.

During lunch an hour later, I told Nathan about the choir director's assignment. His response was a peculiar silence before he quietly said, "You never know . . . you two might actually get along . . . " Then he spent the rest of the time talking excitedly about the ride-along he was scheduled to do that night as part of the paramedic program. I tried to listen intently, to share his enthusiasm about this piece of his life that was obviously very important to him, but then—and for the rest of the day—my plans with Dana Cullen stayed foremost in my thoughts . . . unnerving me.

But that evening, as Dana and I drove from my house to the mall, she started commenting about everything that was wrong with her car, and I began to relax. We talked about running shoes, about the disgusting colors that seemed to be "in" lately, about fast food.

Inside the mall, Dana noticed my blouse and nodded approvingly. "You know," she said, "for someone who can hardly see, you have excellent taste."

Somewhat offensive . . . but a compliment nonetheless. It was probably the best that Dana Cullen could do, considering her superiority complex, so I accepted it. "Thanks."

We walked quickly through the mall toward the court where the recital was to be held. Dana didn't behave as if she felt uncomfortable about having to be seen with me, but I knew that she had to be. People were staring.

SNOW

Suddenly, Marcy Stein, one of the students I knew from the Resource Room I was required to visit once a week because of my "Special Needs Student" status, approached us.

"Hi, Stephanie," she called loudly. "What'ya doing here?"

"Going to a piano recital," I told her. I looked at Dana, who looked back at me, mortified. If there was a student at Canyon Street High who was laughed at more than I was, it was Marcy Stein. But Marcy only had to put up with it in the hallways because she never attended Regular-Ed classes.

"I'm shopping." Marcy pulled something out of the bag she was carrying and held it in my face. "See? I got some new socks."

"Mm-hmm." I stepped back, disgusted with myself for feeling embarrassed by Marcy, but much more concerned with what Dana must be thinking. "We're kind of in a hurry, Marcy," I said. "I'll see you Monday, okay?"

"Okay, Stephanie. See you Monday." Marcy stuffed her new socks back in the sack and walked away from us.

"She's so weird," Dana whispered, and then she laughed. " 'I got some new socks.' Please! Who cares?"

Normally, I would have plowed into someone with an attitude like that with an attitude of my own, but I didn't want to lose whatever ground I may have made with Dana on account of Marcy. So I only mumbled, "She can't help it."

"Sad, huh?" Dana laughed again. "What a loser!"

I said nothing.

I was the loser, I thought as we kept walking. Thinking that I had a right, because I was with someone like Dana Cullen, to treat someone like Marcy the way I had. As if I, or Dana, or anyone else was so great.

Knowing that I could and would apologize to Marcy first thing Monday morning was no comfort at all. I'd just been the same kind of jerk to her that "normal" kids had always been to me. And for the same reason!

I'd always thought that I would do better . . . *be* better . . . given the chance to be among the popular.

But I hadn't. I'd behaved just like everyone else.

Suddenly I recalled something Pastor Ewen had said the first time I'd heard him preach. *"We all sin. That is one thing that has remained constant throughout all generations of humanity."*

We all sin.

But how had I allowed myself to "sin" in the very same manner in which others constantly "sinned" against me? I knew how it felt to be teased. I knew how it felt to be the person embarrassed by someone I thought was my friend—just because I was different and she was with someone "cool." I knew how it hurt. And yet . . . I had done it to Marcy.

Stupid. Spineless.

Sinful.

I prayed silently that God would forgive me, and then I vowed never to respond that way again.

I realized as Dana and I sat on a stone bench at the edge of the court that I had learned more about myself during the past month than I had in all the years previous. And I realized that when I considered *me* in the context of a universe with a God, I wasn't all that impressive, or together, or mature. In the context of a universe with a God, I was a sinner. Just like everyone else.

"But there's good news . . . " Pastor Ewen had said.

I knew what that good news was. And for the first time, I knew that I needed—and wanted—to embrace it.

The question was, would *He* embrace me?

Chapter Seventeen

Mom had already gone to bed by the time Dana dropped me off at home. But Dad was still up, so I asked him to sit up with me awhile. He seemed genuinely glad to. And curious. He covered Shakespeare's cage with a blanket before sitting beside me on the couch. "So . . . how was the recital?"

I shrugged. "Okay."

"Did everything go all right with Dana?"

"Mm-hmm." I supposed that the fact that it really had gone all right with Dana shouldn't have surprised me as much as it did. People were often nicer to me when their friends weren't around.

But that wasn't what I wanted to talk about.

"Dad," I began, and then I stopped. I knew what I was feeling. I knew why. What I didn't know was how to communicate it to my father. I'd just have to try, I decided; that's all. I grabbed a throw pillow and hugged it against my stomach. "Do you remember that sermon Pastor Ewen gave about all of us being sinners?" I asked him.

He nodded.

"I can see now that that's true. I mean, that there's no way anyone is going to ever be perfect on his own."

Again, Dad nodded.

I told him about the incident at the mall with Marcy Stein. "You'd think that me of all people would never do that to someone," I said. "But I did. It makes my stomach hurt all over again every time I think about it."

Half expecting my father to gently remind me that everyone makes mistakes and then warn me not to be too hard on myself, I paused. But he said nothing.

"Anyway," I went on, "I want to believe that Jesus will forgive me . . . for that and all the other junk I've done wrong . . . and I guess I do believe that He can. I just . . ."

I had to admire my father during my uncertain and confused silence after that. He didn't leap forward to seize this opportunity to convince and convert me. He didn't try to supply words for me about how I was feeling. He just waited, apparently content to let whatever was happening inside me happen.

Strangely, though, I began to wish that he would say something.

Finally, he did. "Jesus will forgive you, Stephanie. But there's more to being a Christian than just that."

That I had not expected. "What do you mean?"

"Let's say you buy a house," he said. "You go through before you move in, cleaning, painting, repairing. You expect it to do certain things. To keep you dry when it's raining. To keep you warm when it's blizzarding outside. To shelter you. To be home." He turned a bit to look straight at me. "It's just like that when Jesus comes into our lives."

I nodded. "So you're saying it'll change me . . . like it's changed you?"

"Yes. Because God and sin don't go together." He paused. "And He paid a big price for us, Stephanie."

His death on the cross.

A huge price.

"So it's like He bought me . . . " I muttered, more to myself than to my father.

My father quickly nodded to let me know I'd gotten it right. "There's two things to remember. God expects certain things of you once you're His. But just like us when we buy a house, or whatever, He keeps up on us. He's the one that makes us able to do what He has in mind for us to do."

"Like . . . if you didn't repair the roof after that hailstorm," I said, "it would eventually stop keeping rain off our heads."

"Exactly." Dad smiled. "And I expect my house to keep rain off my head."

I placed the pillow back in the corner of the couch and stood up to stretch. Everything my father had said made sense . . . it seemed logical enough. But I wondered how it could really work with someone who might not always want God "keeping up" on her. A house didn't have any choice. If Dad wanted to fix the roof, he'd fix it. No lip from the house! I suspected it could be a lot more difficult for God.

But then, I doubted that He was the type to give up.

"Okay." I turned to face my father, but I stayed standing. "You're saying that if I want the benefit of having my sin forgiven, I also have to be willing to make room for Jesus in my life?"

"Yes. That's basically what I'm saying." For several moments, he stayed quiet, staring up at me but saying nothing. Then, he said, "Stephanie, you said yourself that you've met Christians who weren't really any different than everyone else. I'm not saying that Jesus doesn't forgive them anymore because they're not making room for Him. But I bet you they're miserable inside." He paused. "I know I am whenever I fight God."

I had to grin. "He's a lot bigger than you are."

"Yes, He is." Dad put his arm around my shoulders when I sat beside him again, and pulled me close. "The thing is, Stephanie, everything He does in our lives—even the things that hurt when He does them . . . the things He asks us to give up, or to start doing, or to stop saying—is out of love for us. Because

He knows what He's created us to be and do, and He's making us into that. One day at a time. Step by step."

I shook my head. "That might be true for people like Pastor Ewen, or Rebekah, or you, but what is God going to use me for? I mean, get real, Dad. What could I ever do for Him?"

"Stephanie," he said, "I guarantee that if you make yourself available to Him and let Him answer that question with your life, you will be amazed. There's nothing special about Pastor Ewen or Rebekah or me that won't be special about you, too, when you let Him work through you." He turned his head to look intently at me. "He uses everyone who comes to Him. People who were raised in the church . . . people who weren't. People who've been saved out of drugs, crime, the occult, empty religions . . . you name it; people have gotten saved out of it, and God has used them. He uses "normal" people *and* people who have cancer, or are in wheelchairs, or are blind, or deaf, or have no arms." He smiled. "Do you really think your head of white hair is going to be an obstacle to Him?"

"Okay, okay, Dad," I said, laughing a little. "I get the point."

And did I ever!

"Still," I said, "it's hard to believe that I could be valuable to God when the only people I've ever been valuable to are you and Ma."

"First of all, that's not true, and you know it," Dad said gently.

I nodded. I did know it. If nothing else, I'd made the track coach at the blind school a very happy man more than once! And there were others: Nathan, my friends at the blind school, the kids I'd worked with the past few summers at a camp for blind children in Vermont, and . . . well, lots of people, now that I'd stopped to think about it.

"Second," Dad said, "the only thing that makes a person truly valuable anyway is God inside of him or her."

I recalled a conversation I'd had recently with Rebekah about that. About how the apostle Paul had come to consider everything that he had done and been before he came to know Christ as being rubbish. Garbage. And about the Bible saying that without God, people in their best state are like a pile of filthy rags.

We're all sinners.

"And third," Dad said, "I think you're going to find that it'll be some of the things about yourself that you think are the most ugly and worthless that God will turn around and use to bring even more glory to Himself through you."

That I couldn't be so sure about . . . but I didn't say so to my father. He'd been right about everything else he'd said tonight. He was probably right about this too.

"So," Dad asked quietly, "are you wanting to be His?"

To be His.

The possibility of me belonging to, being truly accepted by, and even being used by God—the One who'd made the mountains and the oceans and thunderstorms—was almost too overwhelming to accept. But I accepted it anyway.

Chapter Eighteen

Nathan, Judah, and Rebekah arrived at 5:00 the next morning. I wasn't sleeping when Rebekah knocked at the door, but I had forgotten, until I was halfway down the stairs, about our plan to drive to the mountains. It had been our way of denouncing the whole Prom-Thing. While everyone else would be getting their hair done, or renting tuxedos, or buying corsages, we would be exploring an old mine. And while everyone else was at the dance, we would be back in town, eating pizza somewhere.

I opened the door and stepped back to let Rebekah in. "I'm sorry," I said. "I guess I forgot it was today we were going. Let me run up and get dressed."

Rebekah smiled. "We'll be in the Jeep."

I was so excited to tell them that my father had prayed with me to accept Christ that I barely managed to get my hair braided and my hiking boots tied up before I ran back downstairs, left a note for my parents—in case they too had forgotten about my plans—and hurried outside.

It seemed perfect that I was going to be spending this whole day with Nathan, Judah, and Rebekah . . . and the other youth group kids who were going to be meeting us at the church. Friends. Christians.

"I can't believe I forgot about this," I said as I climbed in beside Nathan and pulled the back passenger-side door shut. And I really couldn't believe it. Until last night, any plans I'd made with Nathan Ewen had been the all-and-all of my conscious mind. "Thanks for waiting."

"It wasn't a problem," Judah assured me.

"Good," I said. And then I told them about my visit to the mall with Dana, about running into Marcy there and about how badly I had treated her, about the conversation afterwards with my father, and about my prayer to accept Christ. I knew that I was probably speaking too quickly for them to make sense of all of it, but I couldn't slow myself down.

When I finally finished talking, which wasn't until we turned the corner into the church parking lot, all three of them congratulated me—and it did feel awkward to be receiving such enthusiastic approval for something Someone else had done. But I understood that this was their way of celebrating with me, and I welcomed it.

All four kids in the other four-wheel drive—Michael Kramer, his brother Tony, Natalie Potts, and Levi Jorgensen, someone who was even newer at the church than I was—were excited to hear my news as well.

We stood in the parking lot for several minutes, talking, and eating the hard-boiled eggs and muffins Natalie had brought for breakfast. Then we prayed for the trip, got back into our vehicles, and drove west out of town.

The grasslands, the foothills, the mountains . . . they all looked exceptionally beautiful this morning. A cloudless blue sky. Bright morning sunshine reaching down through the trees, making their green seem even greener than it usually did. Shadows and sunlight stretching across the highway. Even the thirty miles of dusty gravel road and then the bumpy four-wheel drive road switchbacking up the side of a mountain didn't bother me this morning.

The day was gorgeous. Perfect.

"Look at the lakes." Rebekah rolled down her window to point down into the valley.

Even I could see them. Two ovals of deep blue surrounded by rock and pine trees.

"Did you put the fishing poles in?" Nathan asked his brother.

"Yeah. Maybe we'll have time to stop on the way down."

Personally, I couldn't think of a more boring way to spend a couple of hours, but I suspected that not even fishing could ruin this day.

"How did you find out about this road, Judah?" Rebekah asked after we'd turned off the main four-wheel drive road onto a worn and nearly overgrown track.

He shrugged. "I took it once. Last summer."

"It doesn't look like it's very frequently traveled," Rebekah said.

"Those roads go to the best places." Judah slowed down to crawl the Jeep over a huge boulder.

I wasn't sure if it was the trees leaning, or us, as we kept driving up and up. Finally, we turned out of the forest and onto a third trail that looked as if it had nowhere to go but straight up the side of the mountain.

Rebekah pulled in a deep breath and then turned to look out the back window. "You'd better slow down," she cautioned. "We're leaving Michael farther and farther behind us."

Judah laughed. "I'm doing . . . what . . . four miles an hour?"

"He'll catch up," Nathan assured Rebekah. "He's probably staying back on purpose so he doesn't have to breathe our exhaust."

"We'll stop and wait for them," Judah said. He drove until we came to a fork in the road. Go left, and you keep going up the mountain, past the tree line and into the snow. Mercifully, Judah turned right, and we headed down into a small valley dotted with the slumped and graying remains of old miners' cabins. We passed slowly by crumbling claim entrances and pools of rust-colored water, then stopped in front of a huge mine entrance.

"Can you imagine living up here?" Rebekah asked nobody in particular. She stepped out onto the rocky ground. "Especially during winter!"

I grabbed my jacket and joined Rebekah outside. Even now, near the end of May, the peaks above us were still buried in snow. Cold air seemed to roll down them and get caught in the valley. Runoff from the snow above us sounded like a roaring creek. And the sound seemed to come from everywhere. From the trees all around us and even from beneath the boulders we were standing on.

No, I couldn't imagine living here. Especially in a less-than-insulated log cabin with a dirt floor and at best a wood stove for heat. Gold seekers of a century ago had been a rugged bunch, no question.

I heard the rumbling of Michael's extended cab pickup making its way up the loose rocks that someone saw fit to call a road. But I couldn't see it, except in glimpses when the sun reflected off what had to be the two fog lights Michael had mounted to his grill guard. Judah, Nathan, and Rebekah had seen him long before I could, of course, and were already stepping away from the road to make room for him to park.

"Nice road, Ewen." Michael's tone was relaxed enough, but the tense way in which he jumped out of his pickup and slammed the door made me wonder if he was a little shaken. I would have been if I'd had to drive that road . . . even if I could see!

"Sorry," Judah said, and he obviously meant it. "The road's no trouble for me, but you do have a longer wheelbase. I can see where some of those corners could have been interesting."

"Interesting?" Natalie shook her head. "Try terrifying!"

Judah apologized again, and then all five boys surrounded Michael's pickup and inspected the underside, all the while talking about skid plates and axles and clearance and torque.

"So you've never been to these mines either?" I asked Rebekah and Natalie while we waited for the boys to grow bored of cartalk or, failing that, to get hungry and rejoin us.

"Nope," Rebekah said. "Want to go have a look around while we wait for them?"

"Sure," I said.

Natalie said that anything would be better than standing around listening to Tony Kramer recite the benefits of owning a winch.

So, after calling to Judah that we'd be exploring the cabins, Rebekah led the way down a steep rocky slope toward the first graying building in the trees. "Places like this make me want to write a book," she said.

"Not me," I said. "Talk about a life of daily toiling. 'Today I went alone to the mine again because Jack still hasn't shown up. I dug in the dirt and rock all day, to find not one speck of gold. Then I returned to my cabin for a supper of gamy venison stew and stale biscuits. Then I went to bed.'"

"A good writer could make it interesting," Rebekah said. "There were avalanches, wild animals, friendly Indians to trade with and hostile ones to fear. Besides, sometimes they did find gold." She pulled at a shutter that was hanging only by a nearly-rusted-through hinge on the outside of the cabin. "Don't you wonder who the people who lived here were . . . what they were like . . . what they ate for dinner?"

I recalled the supposedly true and grisly story of an old miner in the Beartooth Mountains up in Montana—a Mr. Johnson. His mining partner had been killed by Indians at their claim while Mr. Johnson was away getting supplies. So he found out exactly which Indians had killed his friend and hunted them down. When he found the killer, he cut out the man's liver while he was still alive and ate it in front of him. From then on, Johnson's given first name was forgotten, and Liver Eatin' Johnson became a feared and living legend.

"I wonder how many women came up here to mine with their husbands," Natalie said.

"Not many," I assured her.

We ducked under the split door frame and stepped onto a rotting wood plank floor. There was a window with no glass in it on one wall. An old "table" in the middle of the room. A shelf on the wall beside the door. A rusted bucket on the floor. The roof had fallen in, so sunlight filled what otherwise must have been a very dark place. Wind pressed through the cracks between the logs, whistling where the mud or whatever had been used to seal them had rotted away. There was dirt everywhere, and the smell of age. And flies.

No. The place did not make me want to write a book. Neither did any of the other cabins we investigated. But I did catch myself wanting to picture what the place must have looked like when it was first built. I wanted to hear the voices of the miners and to smell the dust of the rock that had been picked or blown away that day.

"The main mine's right there," Rebekah said. "I've got Judah's flashlight. Shall we have a look?"

"Is it safe?" I asked.

She shrugged. "There's only one way to find out."

As we approached the entrance to the mine, Natalie said, "Maybe we should wait for the boys."

"Most of these mines have been boarded over," Rebekah said, "or they're so caved in that you can't get in anyway."

But this particular mine was neither boarded up nor caved in.

"Wow," Rebekah whispered. She shone the flashlight into a hole that went straight into the side of the mountain. "I've never seen one so intact before."

Carefully, I stepped over a pile of rocks to stand beside her. Her flashlight beam reached into a tunnel that had obviously been carved into the rock by more than hand tools and sheer determination. Wood boards had been wedged a few feet apart up against the roof of the tunnel, I supposed for support, though it didn't look as if this rock was going to go anywhere . . . and if it ever did, a few wood planks certainly wouldn't deter it. There was still half a mountain above our heads!

"The old track along the floor is the only thing that looks like it has weathered during the past century," Rebekah said. She raised the flashlight and shone it farther into the tunnel. "It goes in a long way, looks like." She crouched slightly and stepped forward. "Let's go."

I started to follow Rebekah, but Natalie grabbed my arm. "I don't think we should go in there without the guys."

"Why not?"

"Well . . . they won't know where we are."

Rebekah turned toward the tunnel again. "They'll figure it out. Besides, the last time I looked up the hill, Michael was on his back underneath the truck. He might have found a ding on the transfer case, or something." She laughed. "As if I even know what a transfer case is!"

The transfer case was the part between the transmission and the drive shaft that converted the power into both the front and rear axle on a four-wheel drive. If it had been damaged, getting the truck safely back down the mountain would be a considerable challenge. This was definitely not a two-wheel drive road. But I didn't mention that to Rebekah and Natalie, since we really had no idea what Michael was looking at underneath his truck. But I did say, "They could be up there a while yet. No sense standing out here doing nothing."

"Yeah, but . . . what if there are bears in there?"

Bears?

Rebekah backed out of the tunnel. "Are there bears in these mountains?"

"Black bears, I've been told," I said. "But I've never seen one . . . though that's not saying much!"

Rebekah laughed but did not reenter the tunnel. "Okay, Natalie. We'll wait for the guys."

"I don't mean to be a baby," Natalie said. "I'm just not completely comfortable about going in there. Especially by ourselves."

"It's okay." Rebekah sat on a boulder just outside the entrance to the mine. "Looks like they're coming now, anyway."

The boys toured the cabins much more quickly than we had. When they joined us, Judah took the flashlight from Rebekah and shone it into the mine.

"Are we going to go in?" Levi asked.

Judah shook his head. "It could be dangerous."

Levi bent to look. "It looks all right to me."

"Right here, maybe," Natalie said. "But who knows what's inside."

"Oh, come on." Levi straightened up. "We've got the flashlight. Let's see how far in we can get."

"It would be fun to explore," Nathan agreed.

Judah looked at Rebekah.

She shrugged. "We can always turn around."

Judah tapped the flashlight against his palm a couple of times, and then slowly stepped past the entrance. "Do you have a flashlight in your pickup?" he asked Michael. "It would be good to have more than one."

Michael shook his head.

"Okay," Judah said. "Well . . . stay close."

"What about bears?" Natalie asked, staying back.

"I don't think we have to worry about them here," Judah said.

And that settled it.

Single file, with some of us needing to crouch more than others, and some of us crouching more than we needed to, we entered the mine. It stayed straight for a while, allowing us to enjoy the extra light from the entrance. But the path began to gradually slope downhill, and it wasn't very long until the bright beam from Judah's flashlight was the only light we had.

"You put new batteries in there, right?" Nathan, who was right behind me, called ahead to his brother.

"Yeah."

We walked.

The air began to feel damp and to smell like the mud under your fingernails after you've weeded the flowerbed without gardening gloves on, but the temperature seemed to remain constant. Judah was careful to shine the light back every once in a while so we could all navigate what remained of the track on the floor without breaking our ankles.

"Look," he said, shining his light at a faded arrow marked on the wall. "I've seen a couple of them already. They point the way out."

"There must be other tunnels coming into this one if they marked them," Nathan said.

Though this clearly intrigued Nathan, it frightened me. A straight path was one thing, even in the dark. But a maze of tunnels?

We have a flashlight, I reminded myself. And arrows on the walls.

Rebekah stopped suddenly in front of me and grabbed the back of Judah's sweatshirt. "Did you hear that?"

"It's water dripping somewhere," I told her. "I've been hearing it since we started."

"Really? That was the first time I noticed it."

"I still can't hear it," Judah said.

"I can," Michael said, "now that you pointed it out."

"Watch your step," Judah warned. "Here's our first intersecting tunnel." He stood by the other tunnel as each of us walked past him, shining his light into it. It too seemed to go in forever. The beam faded before it reached any walls.

"This is great!" Nathan whispered.

Judah agreed. "I didn't even think about coming in when I was here last time because I didn't have a flashlight, but I could tell it went in a long way." He stepped carefully over a fallen ceiling beam and then held the light on it for the rest of us. "Anyone else want to lead?"

"I will," Michael volunteered, and eagerly took the flashlight when Judah held it out to him. "Okay, folks, the year is 1847 and my name is Leather Hands MacMannus. This here's my mine. I've got forty men workin' under me, and I reckon we've hauled out . . ."

Michael stopped walking and talking. One by one, we stepped out onto a crisscrossing of tracks that connected a circle of seven or eight tunnels. Like the hub of a wheel connects the spokes. The ceiling was higher here, and there were arrows on every wall leading to the tunnel we'd just come out of. I raised my arms above my head and stretched my back. What a relief to stand straight again!

"Who wants to pick which tunnel we go in?" Michael asked.

"I say we go back," said Natalie.

Rebekah agreed. So did Tony.

"Oh, come on," Levi said. "The tunnel's in great shape. There's no reason to turn around."

"Well," I said, "if we're going to keep going, let's just go straight so we don't have to try and remember which way we turned."

"There are arrows." Nathan's tone held just a hint of scolding.

"You're right." I backed down. "Sorry."

Michael spun in a circle several times and chose a tunnel at random. We turned left into it, and I vowed to myself that I'd be the one to remember that we'd have to turn right on the way back out.

"We'll just go a little ways," Judah promised Natalie and Rebekah. "Okay?"

Rebekah gave her okay immediately. Natalie, however, hesitated.

Judah called to Michael. "Wait. We shouldn't do this if not everyone wants to."

"Thanks, Judah," Natalie said, "but I'm okay with it, I guess."

"It's not like we can get lost," Nathan said, and even I could see the quick glare his big brother gave him in response.

We walked deeper and deeper into the second tunnel. I noticed moisture on the walls and ceiling in several places, and the odor of dampness was much more pungent than it had been in the first tunnel. There were puddles on the floor, turning the rock slippery and the wood that remained of the track waterlogged and soggy. It felt as if we were stepping on rotting watermelon rinds. "There could be rats in here," I said. "They like dank places, and this is definitely getting more and more dank."

"Oh, it's just a little wat—" Michael's words caught in his throat as he started to fall forward.

Plastic and glass crashed to the rock floor, and the shrill sound echoed in the tunnel. Then came the splintering crunch of cracking wood as something heavy landed on it. . . . And then, blackness.

Chapter Nineteen

"Where's the light!?"

"Turn on the light!"

"I'm looking for it," Judah said. "Everyone else stay where you are."

"It's pitch-black in here," Natalie said.

"No kidding," Nathan snapped.

"Everyone relax," Judah scolded. "I've got the flashlight . . . part of it . . . Michael, are you all right?"

"Yeah. I think so."

"What happened? Did you slip?"

"Uh, huh."

"Quit talking and find the rest of the flashlight, will you?" Tony Kramer demanded.

"I'm working on it," Judah promised him, somewhat impatiently.

"Sorry."

I heard the sound of several tiny pieces of glass being further crushed against rock as something came down on them.

"I found the rest of the flashlight," Judah said dully.

"It's broken," Michael said. "I just yanked a piece of the lightbulb out of my arm."

"Are you bleeding?" Nathan asked, and then I felt him move past me toward the sound of Michael's voice.

"Yeah."

After a few moments of complete silence, Nathan said, "Okay . . . okay. I need something . . . something long enough to wrap around his arm a few times and then tie tight."

"Anyone have a pocket knife?" I asked. When I felt a nudge at my shoulder, from whom I didn't know, I reached back until I had his knife in my hand. The first lever I pulled up was a nail clipper. Then I found the fishing line cutter. Then the knife. With it, I carefully cut a strip off around the entire bottom of my T-shirt, which I then held out into the darkness. "Here, Nathan."

It took a moment, but he did eventually find the cloth and grab it out of my hand. Then we waited while he first wrapped it around Michael's arm and then tied it. I could tell when he'd finished by the sound of the cloth rubbing and being pulled hard against itself.

"Is he all right?" Judah asked.

"It's bleeding pretty good," Nathan said, "but that should keep it until we get out of here."

"How are we going to get out of here?" Natalie sounded ready to cry. Or scream. "We have no light!"

As calmly as if he were telling someone how he planned to spend his first week out of school after graduation, Judah said, "We're just going to go back the way we came until we get to the hub and then . . . and then we'll——"

"Turn right," I said.

"Exactly," Judah said. "We'll turn right."

"Piece of cake," Nathan said.

"Yeah," agreed Michael. "Cake."

"Okay," Judah said, "you're going to turn around." He waited while we did. "Now you're going to put your left hand on the wall and your right hand out in front of your face a couple of inches.

And you're going to walk. Slowly. Test each step before you put your weight down on it." He paused. "Okay?"

I smiled. Judah had stepped forward to be exactly what we needed someone to be to get us moving. Someone to take charge. Someone to act as if this was going to be nothing more than a walk down the hall to the school cafeteria.

Someone to step out first into the darkness.

We walked. Slowly. Step after step after step. And every step was work.

"I feel like I can't breathe," Tony said after a while.

"There's just as much air in here as there was when we had light, Tony," I said. But I, too, was beginning to feel smothered by the stale and humid blackness. "It's just your mind thinking it's different."

"Let's sing something," Rebekah suggested.

So we sang something. One verse of a church chorus. Two verses. Three. And still, we hadn't reached the hub. Nobody could remember the words to the fourth verse, and nobody suggested another song.

We walked.

"How's the arm, Michael?" Nathan asked.

"Good," Michael answered.

"Tell me if you start feeling dizzy, or anything," Nathan said.

"I said it's good."

The fingers of my left hand brushed lightly along the cold rock wall as I moved forward. I thought about so many people I knew at the school for the blind who lived in this kind of darkness all the time. No light. No color. No clue about what lay ahead of them except what they'd memorized beforehand. And unlike the eight of us in this mine who were sharing the blackness, my totally blind friends had to live in it alone while everyone sped by them in the light. Also unlike the eight of us, most totally blind people didn't have any end of the mine to look forward to. No future hope of rejoining, or joining for the first time, the world of the seeing.

But they didn't have to remain in blackness about eternity, I realized, and determined that as soon as I got home that night, I would start writing letters to them about the Savior who was waiting to embrace and love them.

"Okay," Judah said, "we're at the hub."

"Switch hands and put your right hand on the wall," I said. "Follow it to the next tunnel." Then I froze. We hadn't gone into the first tunnel on the left when we'd crossed the hub. We'd passed by one . . . or two. I tried to remember . . . but couldn't. I'd been so focused on remembering which direction we'd turned that I hadn't thought to count the number of tunnels between the one to the entrance and the one we'd turned into . . . I supposed because in the back of my mind I'd figured we wouldn't need to know any of that—with arrows plainly marking the way out. I swallowed, but my mouth had gone dry. "Did anyone pay attention to how many tunnels we walked by before turning into this one?"

Silence.

"Two, I think," Rebekah said.

Levi said that he thought we'd only passed by one.

"I didn't realize we'd passed any," Tony said.

"We definitely did," I said. "I just can't remember how many."

"I can't either," Judah admitted.

"Now what do we do?" Natalie sounded ready to panic again . . . and this time Judah wasn't going to have a reassuring answer for her.

We stood in the hub for several minutes, none of us speaking, none of us moving. Finally, Judah said, "Well, we have to pick one and keep moving. That's all we can do. We're definitely not going to get out if we stand around here."

"He's right," I said. "I know that we passed by at least one tunnel, so let's skip one and go in the next one."

"But what if we passed by two?" Nathan wanted to know. "Or even three?"

"We'll figure out it's the wrong tunnel, turn around, and try the next one, and the next one if we have to, until we get out." Judah started walking. "Let's go."

"But *how* will we figure out it's the wrong tunnel?"

"I don't know, Nathan," Judah said. "We won't get to the entrance?"

"We'll know before then," I said, trying my best to sound calm. The situation was tense enough. If we started allowing ourselves to take our fear out on one another, it would only make things worse. "We'll . . . pray, or something. Let's just go."

Nobody wanted to move, including me. But even less did I want to stay in the dark hub of this mine until I died of thirst. So I followed Judah.

"Here's the first tunnel," he said.

Within seconds, my right hand was reaching out into empty air. Without the rock wall to touch, the next few steps were frightening and disorienting. But Judah had stopped at the opposite wall of the tunnel and said, "It's right here," just as my hand hit rock again.

"Thanks," I said, and then I did the same for the person behind me . . . who signaled the person behind her . . . person to person until all eight of us had passed by the vacant hole of the tunnel. Then, one by one, we turned into the next one.

"Please let this be the tunnel out," Rebekah whispered behind me.

But within moments, I knew it wasn't. I couldn't place the difference, exactly, but I knew that this tunnel was not the one we'd come out of. "We need to turn around," I told Judah.

"Why?"

"I . . . I don't know. It just feels different," I said.

Judah kept walking. "It's because we have no light," he said.

"Maybe." I knew that it was more than that. But since I couldn't say the smell wasn't right, or it echoed differently, or the ground was too muddy or sloped too much, or anything specific, I kept my mouth shut and followed him.

Five minutes in. Ten.

"Are you still doing all right, Michael?" Nathan asked.

"Yeah."

"You make sure you tell me if you start—"

"I will," Michael impatiently promised.

I stopped walking. I'd figured out what was different about this tunnel. "Judah, we need to turn around."

"We should go a little further, Stephanie. We haven't come far enough to reach the entrance if this is the right—"

"Listen to me!" I felt as if I'd never be able to explain quickly enough. I stretched out my hand to grab him by the arm, but he'd gotten just far enough ahead of me to be out of my reach. "Feel how the air is colder in here, Judah? And how it kind of feels like it's being sucked away from us? That means—"

In the next instant, as my mouth hung open with words still in it but no voice to say them, Judah found out what it meant.

Chapter Twenty

As quickly as I could, I got to my hands and knees, and then to my stomach. Judah had yelled out for only a second, and that scared me. "I need some help up here!"

"What happened?"

"Get on your hands and knees and get up here, Nathan! Hurry!"

"Why do I have to—?"

"Just do it!" I got to the end of the rock floor ahead of Nathan, and though I was terrified to do it, I called to Judah.

"I'm here," he yelled up to me.

Thinking that he must have somehow turned himself around to grab hold of the edge of the rock wall, and convinced by the fear and strain in his voice that he wasn't going to be able to hold on for more than a couple of seconds, I felt frantically along the rock and even leaned over the edge as much as I dared, but I couldn't find his hands. "Keep talking, Judah! Where are you?"

What if he'd fallen too far down for any of us to reach him?

"Here! There's nothing over here to grab onto, Stephanie!"

Over here?

That was it. That was why I couldn't find him. He hadn't turned around. Somehow he'd fallen out forward instead of straight down and had been able to grab the other side of the shaft!

But that meant that he was across the hole from us.

How would we ever get to him?

I crawled to my left to determine whether there was a ledge against the wall between this side of the hole and Judah's side. A loose rock slipped into the hole, and it wasn't until several still seconds later that I heard it hit water somewhere down below us.

"Hold on, Judah!"

By this time, Nathan and Tony had both crawled up beside me and had figured out what had happened.

"What can we do?" Tony asked.

"We've got to get around to him," Nathan said. "How far across do you think it is?"

He was asking me. How did he expect me to know that? I hoped he wasn't thinking about jumping across . . .

Nathan told Judah to talk and keep talking.

"Nathan," I said, "there is absolutely no way of knowing if this tunnel keeps going on the other side of this hole! You might just smack yourself into another rock wall and end up in the same position as Judah . . . maybe worse off!" But even as I spoke, I knew that there was no other option but for Nathan to try to jump across. Nobody had a rope. The edges along the walls to the left and right side of the hole were barely an inch wide—not nearly wide enough for someone to try to cross over on. The hole was too wide to straddle, even if someone did think that an inch for each foot might be sufficient.

"It sounds like it's about five feet across," Nathan said. "I can do that. And I don't think there's a wall there. I mean, wouldn't there be an echo if there was? Wouldn't it feel smaller in here than it does?"

"Hurry!" Judah shouted.

"I've got to try!" Nathan got to his feet.

I held my breath. Behind me, Rebekah held hers. All of us did.

Nathan jumped.

What if he didn't go far enough? What if he did, and then lost his balance on the other side? What if he hit his head on the ceiling of the opposite tunnel? What if there was a wall there? What if . . .

"I'm across!" Nathan shouted.

A unanimous shaky breath came from the six of us still on this side of the hole.

"Where are you, Judah?" Nathan slapped the side of the rock wall and kept slapping it until he said, "Okay, I've got you!" and then struggled for several seconds to pull his brother safely up and onto the edge. "Are you all right?" he asked Judah.

"Is he all right?" Rebekah wanted to know at the same time.

"I'm all right."

He sounded shaken—and who wouldn't?—but he was unhurt.

After waiting several minutes for his brother to catch his breath, Nathan told us to move away from the edge to make room for them to jump back across.

I had to wonder, as first Nathan and then Judah jumped safely across, if I could have pulled together the nerve to jump across five feet of empty blackness over such a deep hole to an unknown other side. I didn't think so. And Nathan had just done it *twice!*

"Stephanie," Judah said, when we'd all moved several yards away from the hole and back in toward the hub of the mine, "the next time you say it's time to turn around, I'm stopping right then and there!" He paused. "In fact, why don't you lead the rest of the way out?"

"Me?" I shook my head . . . and then realized that nobody could see me doing it. "No. I can't."

"Hey, we're all blind in here," Nathan said. "Maybe, you know, you're a little better at this kind of thing than the rest of us."

"I can see, Nathan," I reminded him.

"Yeah, but I never would have noticed the difference in the way the air was moving back there. And I definitely wouldn't have been able to figure out what it might have meant, even if I did notice it."

"He's right, Stephanie," Judah said. "I walked right into that vertical shaft without even a clue that it was coming."

"Hey, I tried to warn you." I hoped that my smile was evident in my tone since he wouldn't be able to see it on my face.

"I know," he replied quietly. "Which is exactly the point."

"Nathan?"

It was Michael, who was standing right behind me. He sounded ready to fall over. I turned around, grabbed his arm, and slowly helped him sit on the floor. His skin felt cold, but sweaty, and he was shaking.

"I don't feel so good," he said.

Nathan made his way over to where Michael and I were sitting. "Let me check on your arm."

In all the confusion of losing the flashlight and not knowing which tunnel to take, I'd forgotten that Michael had seriously cut his arm. Nathan had not said that the cut was serious, but I'd heard fear in his voice when he'd asked for something to wrap around it and in his frequent questions of Michael about how he was feeling. Fear well-concealed in calmness, but fear nonetheless. "Is he all right?" I asked.

"No. The cloth you gave me is soaked through, and he's still bleeding."

Remembering the knife in my pocket, I pulled it out and, knowing exactly which lever to pull up this time, cut another couple of inches off the bottom of my T-shirt. "Here," I said. "Wrap it again."

"Tighter this time," Nathan muttered to himself as he worked.

"Can he walk?" Judah asked his brother.

"He'll have to," Nathan said. "I'll help him."

"Okay," I said, and then slowly got to my feet. "I'll lead."

Judah gently squeezed my shoulder. "And I'll help Nathan with Michael."

As I started walking again with my right hand on the rock wall and my left hand out a couple of inches in front of my face, I closed my eyes. *Lord Jesus, I didn't expect to be talking to You about my eyesight so soon after believing in You. And I'd expected that when I did talk to You about it, I'd be whining. But I'm not going to whine. I'm just asking that if my poor vision can in any way help us to get out of here, especially now that Michael is hurt, that You will use it.*

Since Nathan and Judah were both using one of their hands to support Michael between them, I tried to mention everything about the trail that might cause a problem for them. The ceiling's a little low here. The wall bends in a bit here on the right. There's a little dip in the floor. Loose wood on the ground—don't trip.

When my right hand followed the rock wall out of the tunnel and into the hub, I felt fear in my stomach like too much pizza too late at night. We didn't have time anymore to wander through all the tunnels until we found the one with the entrance. Michael needed to get out of this mine and off this mountain as quickly as we could get him there. But I still didn't know which tunnel was the right one. What if I chose the wrong one and Michael lost too much blood while we were figuring it out?

Lord, please, help me choose the right tunnel the first time.

I walked along the wall of the hub until I came to the first tunnel. I stepped out a few feet and then just stood there.

Nothing. No hint that this either was or wasn't the right one. No certain smell. No certain level of humidity. Nothing.

I decided to walk to the next tunnel. I knew that we hadn't gone by more than four tunnels on our way in, so I knew that the way out was either the tunnel I'd just stopped at or the next one.

SNOW

When I reached the next opening, I stood silent and still again in front of it.

"Which one?" Nathan asked quietly from behind me.

"I . . . I don't know." *Which one, God?*

Just then I noticed that the hair I'd tucked behind my right ear because it had come loose from my braid was moving . . . just a little . . . just enough to tickle the side of my neck. That had to mean that there was air movement inside this tunnel. Air that was being pushed in toward the hub of the mine. Air that smelled, I realized when I took a few steps into the tunnel, the tiniest bit like pine.

"This one!" I shouted, relieved enough to cry, but refusing to. "This one's the way out!"

And it was.

Chapter Twenty-One

Neither of my parents were home when Judah and Rebekah dropped me off. I walked slowly upstairs to my room, took a long warm shower, and changed clothes. Then I sat on the edge of my bed and stared out the window at nothing. Though I was glad not to have to sit down right away and answer a million questions about everything that had just happened, being alone didn't suit me either. The house seemed too quiet. My emotions seemed too loud. Sitting down to enjoy a mug of hot chocolate while Shakespeare prattled on about the time of day would be out of the question.

Eating wouldn't be, though. I hadn't realized how hungry I was, or that I was hungry at all, until I thought about the leftover scalloped potatoes and ham in the refrigerator downstairs.

The sun was low in the sky by the time I sat on the top step of the back deck with my plate and a glass of iced tea. The evening wasn't warm, but I allowed myself to be calmed anyway by the color of the clouds. The first splashes on the sky spoke of another gorgeous sunset.

I watched for more than an hour, long after I'd finished eating, as the clear western sky turned gold and then rusty and then blue with dusk. I listened to the birds, to a lawn mower in a yard somewhere down the block, and to the traffic. I tried to make sense of a perfect day gone crazy.

I felt awed by the fact that God had used me to get us out of the mine, but let down by the fact that He'd allowed us to become lost in the first place. I felt invigorated by the aftertaste of being part of such an adventure, and yet exhausted by the regret that we didn't have just another ordinary day in the mountains . . . a picnic, four-wheeling, a snowball fight, even fishing. And mostly, I felt unsettled about Michael. Even Natalie had commented that he'd looked as white as me when we finally reached daylight again at the entrance to the mine. And he'd looked even whiter when we brought him into the emergency room an hour and a half later.

My father had been on duty then, and he'd assured me before I left that Michael was already on his way to being fine again . . . but one frightening fact continued to haunt me. If we had taken an hour longer to find the way out of the mine, or had had any kind of trouble on our way down the mountain, or had gotten caught behind the road construction in the eastbound lane instead of being flagged past it, Michael could have bled to death.

The chime of the doorbell and Shakespeare's simultaneous announcement of "Company! Company!" startled me even as it rescued me from my own thoughts. I ran quickly through the house, left my plate on the counter as I passed by it, and pulled open the front door.

"Nathan." I was surprised to see him. He'd told me that he was going to stay at the hospital with Michael. "I was watching the sunset. Come on out to the deck."

"Okay." We walked across the room and out through the sliding glass door. "Good news," he said. "They sent Michael home already."

"Really?"

I sat down on the deck steps and he sat beside me.

"Yep. They said we must have done everything right." He turned to look at me. "I told them that Michael has you to thank."

"Oh, come on, Nathan," I said. "It was you who took care of his arm. And, as far as what I did . . . anyone could have done it if they'd have stopped to pay attention."

"Maybe," he agreed. "But 'anyone' didn't do it. You did."

I pulled my knees up against my chest and rested my chin on them. "You know what's really weird?"

"What?"

"When my father first told me that God could use me . . . well, first off, I didn't believe him! But then I figured that maybe He could, you know, use my sense of humor, or my life experience, or whatever. I never would have thought He'd be able to use—or *want* to use—my handicap." I shook my head. "I hate that word!"

"Nothing handicaps God, Stephanie," Nathan said. "Except maybe our pride—thinking we're too good, or not good enough—that keeps us from making ourselves available to Him." He laughed a little. "And even that doesn't handicap Him from getting His work done. I mean, He's God! It just means He might have to use someone else to do it."

I nodded. I hoped that I would never fail God or rob myself of opportunities to serve Him because of a wrong opinion of myself. It seemed to me as I sat there looking at Nathan—but not really looking at him—that serving God wasn't about *me* at all. It wasn't about who I was, how I'd been raised, what handicaps I had, or even my strengths and weaknesses. It was about Him. Who He is. What He can do . . . and the fact that He chooses to do anything at all with any of us flawed human beings!

He had made me . . . like a potter makes pottery. I hadn't slipped off the wheel in midproduction, half-finished. How could I complain to Him about the way I was?

Dad had read something to me from the Book of Job the night he'd prayed with me to receive Christ. "Just so you'll understand that He's God," he'd said. The passage had made intellectual sense to me then, but it engaged me in a much deeper way now.

Where wast thou when I laid the foundations of the earth? . . . Who shut up the sea with doors? . . . Where is the way where light dwelleth? . . . Hast thou entered into the treasures of

*the snow? . . . Canst thou send lightnings, that they may go, and
say unto thee, Here we are? . . .*

The treasures of the snow. Not only had I never entered them,
I didn't even know for sure what they were!

Nor did I know why I had been born an albino. Whether God
had specifically formed me this way, or had simply allowed it to
occur in Ma's womb, or even if it was nothing more than genet-
ics at work.

It didn't matter.

I was His. And He was God. The One who *had* been there
when the earth's foundations were laid. The One who had entered
into the treasures of the snow and knew exactly what they were
. . . just as He knew everything else.

Just as He knew me.

And He had shown me that even the thing I'd always thought
of as my ugliest characteristic—my physical abnormality—could
be useful with Him. Like the ugly old parking lot rock that had
turned out to not be so ugly after all.

I knew that other people would still tease me . . . and that it
would still hurt. I knew that I wouldn't quickly erase the effects
on my attitude of so many years of feeling inferior. I knew that I
might be tempted to use my "handicap" as an excuse to avoid
doing certain things for God (Lord, I can't go over and say *hi* to
that new kid in youth group! What if he's not a new kid at all, but
one of the old ones with a new haircut?). And I knew that it would
still be a pain to find out how much a hamburger costs at a fast-
food restaurant, to have to take public transportation everywhere,
and to be the one person in a crowd that people can't help notic-
ing.

But I knew too that God could work through, past, or in spite
of all—as long as I always made room for Him. He'd use it just
as He had worked past our broken flashlight, half a mine's worth
of lightless tunnels, a rough four-wheel-drive road at high speed,
and an interstate under construction—to bring Michael to safety.

"That's great news about Michael," I said to Nathan.

"You're not kidding, it's great news!" He stood up. "Judah and Rebekah wanted to know if we wanted to meet them for that pizza we'd planned on?"

"I already ate." I smiled. "But there's always room for a slice of pizza."

He nodded. "And we can run some by the Kramers' for Michael on our way back."

"Sounds good." I stood and stretched the kinks out of my back. "Do you mind waiting a minute or two? There's something I want to do first."

"Sure. I'll be out in the truck."

I waited until the front door closed behind him, then I ran upstairs to my room. First, I dug around in my closet until I found an empty box—the big square box I'd just emptied when I'd taken out the last of five packages of 500 sheets of paper. Then I went to my desk, leaned down, and pulled the T-shirt I'd worn that day out of the trash. I'd thrown it away because after cutting two two-inch strips off all around the bottom to wrap Michael's arm, the shirt was frayed and potentially immodest. But now I had a new plan for it.

After pulling the top off the empty paper box, I carefully folded the shirt and set it inside. Then I placed the top back on and carried the box to my closet, where I lifted it up onto my top shelf—right beside my computer monitor box full of track ribbons and goalball medals. As I stepped back and pulled my closet door shut, I wondered whether I was strange for thinking of the two boxes up there on my shelf as sort of a symbol of my conversion from life without God to life *with* Him.

The first box was full of mementos of all the things *I'd* been able to accomplish with my life, in spite of everything. The second box was the start of what I had no doubt would be a huge collection of keepsakes of the things that God would be able to accomplish with my life, in spite of everything.

Chapter Twenty-Two

One week later, I stood at the line waiting for the start of the state final in the girls' 1600 meter run. I could hear my parents in the stands, along with Nathan—who had just won his race—his whole family, and Michael Kramer and his family all cheering for me. I could hear the footsteps of someone running down the infield straightway for their approach at the long jump. I could feel the tense silence of the runners around me . . . and in my own throat.

All of us waiting for the crisp *crack* of the starter's gun.

This was my last opportunity of the year to defeat Dana Cullen, and I could think of no better time or place to finally accomplish that than here at the state meet.

The next time you're in a race with her, just pretend she's not even there. That's what Nathan had said.

The competition's going to be tougher at state, so I want you to know beforehand that I'm proud of each and every one of you . . . no matter how you finish this weekend. That's what the coach had said.

Run your best race, and you'll be a winner. That's what Dad had said.

And Pastor Ewen? *God won't love you any more or less because you do or don't win.* That's what he'd said.

Great advice, all of it, but all I wanted right now was to put my first foot past the starting line and keep it one step ahead of Dana Cullen's feet until after we'd crossed the finish line.

At the sound of the gun, I bolted. I wasn't interested in playing follow the leader until the final lap. In this race, I wanted to be the leader. My usual strategy had earned me only red ribbons up till now. Today, I wanted the blue one.

We ran.

I caught my hands trying to fist up and relaxed them. I caught my side starting to ache and worked harder to breathe in only through my nose. I caught my mind wondering why I still felt any need whatsoever to beat Dana, and I forced myself to concentrate on the pacing of the two girls nearest me.

Right behind me.

I kept a step ahead of them until the middle of the third lap, when one of them pulled up alongside me.

Dana.

We ran side by side for an entire lap of the track. 200 meters to the finish line. My thighs were burning. My lungs. My shoulders. My mouth had gone sticky and then dry. My breaths felt like sand in my throat. And sweat was dripping into my eyes. But I kept running, knowing that I could pull ahead of Dana, if only for a second, and win the race.

Knowing it.

100 meters from the finish line.

50.

And that's where it happened. A girl in a uniform whose school colors I didn't recognize sprinted by us, beating us to the finish line.

Dana and me? It was impossible for me to know which of us had finished in second place . . . because it seemed as if we'd crossed the line as one runner instead of two, at exactly the same moment.

Minutes passed while we awaited the official results of the race.

"Good run," Dana said to me.

"You too."

We walked together toward the infield, where we both leaned forward with our palms on our knees to catch our breath.

"It's a tie!" Our coach approached us, congratulated each of us with a pat on the back, and then jogged across the infield toward the starting line of the boys' 4×400 meter relay.

A tie.

Second place.

Another red ribbon to drop in my computer monitor box.

"What are your plans for the summer?" Dana asked me. She sat in the grass and stretched forward to touch her toes.

I sat beside her and did the same. "Well, I expect to go along on some four-wheel-driving trips. Then there's youth camp in Wyoming that I plan to go to."

"Is that a church thing?"

I nodded. "This'll be my first year."

"Sounds fun."

"That's what I've heard," I said. "We have youth meetings at our church almost every Saturday night. I've been to those, so I know they're fun." I stopped stretching to sit up straight and look her in the eye—as well as I could, anyway. "You should come sometime."

She kept stretching for several seconds without saying anything. But then, quietly, she said, "Maybe I will. You go to Nathan's dad's church?"

"Yeah."

"He seems really . . . " Dana struggled for a moment for the right word, but finally settled on, "genuine."

"He is," I told her. And then I told her about the first sermon I'd heard him give and about the ways in which learning to accept Christ's love for me had changed my life. About how I'd made it a point since then to tell anyone who laughingly compared my hair color to winter precipitation that "white as snow" isn't a bad way to be . . . especially when you're talking about sins and God's forgiveness. In fact, it's a great way to be . . . maybe you'd like to hear more?

I could have kept talking, too, I was somewhat surprised to discover, but our coach called us over to the stands to cheer for one of our teammates who was set to win or lose the long jump with his final attempt.

"I bet you'll beat me next year," Dana said. She stood up and held her hand out to me. When I'd taken it and she'd pulled me up, she grinned and added, "Once or twice."

It occurred to me then that Dana was probably a lot more disappointed than I was about finishing second in the state meet after winning nearly all of her other races of the season. "That's right," I said. "And next year at state we'll tie for first."

The rest of the meet and our two-hour bus trip back to Canyon Street High sped by, but not nearly as quickly as the girl who'd overtaken Dana and me to win our race. Nathan offered to drive me home after a brief team meeting, and I accepted.

We'd gotten to within two blocks of my house before Nathan spoke. "I'm sorry you didn't beat Dana today," he said.

"You know what? It's no big deal." When he glanced at me with an expression that said *Yeah right, Stephanie* as clearly as words could have, I couldn't help smiling. "I mean it," I said. "At first, yeah, I was disappointed. But then we started talking about God. Somehow, not beating her didn't seem to matter so much after that."

He slowed down to turn into my driveway. "You and Dana talked about God?"

"Yeah."

"That's great." He unbuckled his seat belt so that he could turn to face me. "I'm glad you're not upset about not winning. It was a great race. Besides, beating Dana never should have mattered to you the way it did."

"I know." I nodded slowly. I wasn't embarrassed, exactly, about how obsessed I'd become with the idea that I'd prove myself somehow if I could only run a faster 1600 meters than Dana Cullen, but I wasn't proud of it either. That goal had been my refuge in a frightening new place. My one means of acquiring some supposed value for myself. Or so I'd thought. "I know better now, Nathan," I said.

He smiled. "See you tomorrow morning at church?"

"Definitely." I stepped out of the truck and shut the door.

The evening sun shone warm on my shoulders as I walked up the steps to my front door. One of our neighbors said "hello" to me from her porch. Children were squealing as they ran through a sprinkler in a nearby yard. And someone was barbecuing chicken—I hoped it was Ma!

I called, "I'm home," to my parents and ran upstairs to my room. I couldn't wait to shower and get into clean clothes, but I decided to put away my things first. I threw my shoes in the closet, grabbed my sunscreen and hairbrush out of my gym bag, threw it and the rest of its contents onto my laundry pile, then I reached up to my top shelf for my computer monitor box. Before my hands touched it, though, I'd changed my mind.

The red ribbon I'd won today belonged in my new box, not the old one. Not because I felt that I'd accomplished any more by finishing even with Dana instead of behind her, but because God had made it possible for me to come home content.

Red ribbon instead of blue.

Tied with Dana instead of ahead of her.

Tangled white hair.

And all.

SNOW

I smiled as I placed the ribbon in the box beside the T-shirt I'd worn in the mine, a copy of the three page letter I'd written to one of my friends at the school for the blind—my first "testimony" letter—and the New Believers pamphlet Nathan had taken me through. I could tell already that I was either going to have to quit being a pack rat or get a bigger box . . . because God is a huge God and I had a whole life of being His ahead of me.

I took a quick shower, put on some comfortable clothes, and hurried downstairs just as Ma came in from the back deck with dinner.

Barbecued chicken.

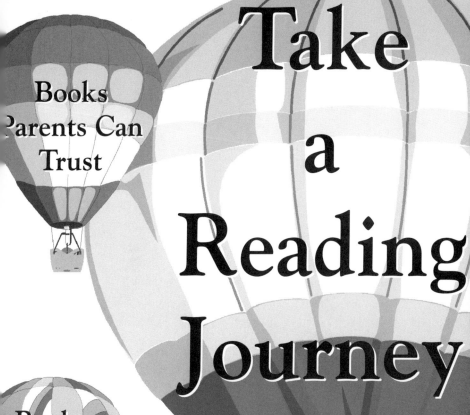

Take a Reading Journey

Books Parents Can Trust

Books Kids Can Enjoy